Yagmar the Barbarian: The Singer and the Staff

Pat Luther

Material originally published to Kindle Vella Copyright ©2023 by Pat Luther

Additional material ©2024 by Pat Luther

ISBN 978-1-7367515-6-5

Cover by Chantel Saban

Interior art by Samantha L. Eno.

All rights reserved.

No portion of this book may be reproduced in any form without written permission from the publisher or author, except as permitted by U.S. copyright law.

For every kid who ever wanted to write stories about their D&D characters.

And every parent and teacher who told them they couldn't.

Contents

1. We All Meet in an Inn — 4
2. An Unexpected Guest — 9
3. A Late Addition — 14
4. A Ring of Power — 22
5. In Search of the Unknown — 27
6. A Rude Awakening — 33
7. An Unfortunate Encounter — 38
8. Blood in the Water — 45
9. Up the Creek — 49
10. On Stranger Shores — 54
11. A Dream of Dragons — 59
12. Ere Break of Day — 66
13. A Dance in Darkness — 71
14. A Song and a Dance — 76
15. Pursuit by Firelight — 81

16.	A Little Night Music	86
17.	An Interlude with Thoughts and Frets	91
18.	Traveling Songs	98
19.	And We're Walking...	107
20.	A Fight on an Ancient Road	113
21.	Death in the Dust	118
22.	Secrets and Lies	123
23.	A Night of Peace and Love	129
24.	Raven's Feast	134
25.	Death from Above	141
26.	Aftermath and Forewarning	147
27.	Descent	153
28.	Melody of a Madman	160
29.	Wards and Warsong	166
30.	Soldiers of Stone	172
31.	Breaking Bonds	178
32.	The Singer and the Staff	185
33.	Death and Betrayal	191
34.	A New Direction	196
35.	Blood in the Snow	202
36.	A Ration of Magic	208

37. Up and Out	214
38. From Snow to Sand, and Dust	220
39. Waiting for an Ambush	225
40. Blood on the Sand	230
41. We All Meet in an Inn	235
42. Fight the Future	241
43. Blood on the Floor	246
44. The Shar'i'nol	251
45. Where There Be Dragons	258
Death of a Young Wizard	266

One
We All Meet in an Inn

"There's a reason so many of your stories start in places like this," said the large man across from me as he unrolled a worn map on the table between us. He took my empty ale tankard and placed it on one end to hold it down then plucked one of the twin throwing axes from his belt and laid it on the other end.

The bench creaked beneath him when he shifted his weight. It did a valiant job of holding him. I supposed it often held that much, but usually spread between two or three people.

Yagmar the Barbarian. I had sung tales of this man since I'd first begun practicing the crwth and grown up hearing even more. As a child, I used to play at *being* him, waving sticks at my siblings after chores.

He wore no armor, unless there was leather under his furs, which he wore in abundance. An enormous axe was slung across his back. I wasn't sure I would have even been able to lift it, let alone fight with it.

Even if I hadn't known who he was, I would have gravitated to him if I had been merely looking for someone who could fight.

And now I had to convince him to join me on a job I didn't want to do for a woman I didn't trust.

The map on the table showed all of Western Torlindl. It was worn and almost illegible in places, but our current location, the town of Tenn, was clearly marked and beautifully rendered. At one end of the map was a large-scale drawing of the free city of Pendwy, situated at the mouth of the River Caber. The map followed the river all the way up to the Yikal Mountains and across the desert past them.

On the far eastern edge was an ornate arrow beneath which was written, "Beyond this point, there be dragons." I wondered if that might actually be true. I suspected this man might know.

Yagmar continued his musings. "Where else are you going to find a clean, flat surface like this? Not to mention unlimited ale and meat, and enough room for a number of us to gather."

I got his point, though I thought he may be straining the definition of clean.

I glanced around the room. Ours was far from the only table in use, though most were covered in plates of food, more tankards, and an occasional drunk, instead of a map that I suspected was older than the one my grandmother had brought home from the war. For as long as I could remember, that map had hung with her sword above the mantle in my home in Granjoriil, far to the North.

The inn was busy. In the three days I'd been there I'd never seen it empty. Tenn was a small city, made prosperous by its position on the confluence of two great rivers, and the Drowning Dragon Inn was one of its largest and most famous landmarks.

Yagmar changed the subject. "You going to tell me about our mysterious employer?"

"Let's wait until the rest get here," I said. "That way I only have to say everything once. Speaking of ale, though..." I drew my dagger and laid it on the map so I could lift my tankard. A harried serving girl came near with a large pitcher. She hurried over and refilled it and I dropped a silver royal onto her tray. She smiled appreciatively, then turned to fill Yagmar's as well.

"Some meat and cheese, too," he told her, "We're expecting more shortly." He dropped another whole silver on her tray, and she hurried off to do his bidding.

While his attention - I thought - was on the girl, I quickly strummed a couple of strings on my crwth, which was sitting on the bench next to me, leaning against the table. While the notes still vibrated audibly, I hummed a counter-tone, shaping the small magic and twisted my thoughts in the right direction to make it do what I wanted. I then took a sip of the suddenly cool ale in my hand. The drink was now at least palatable.

I set it down and Yagmar was staring right at me, with a look of amusement combined with something I couldn't quite finger. Accusation, maybe, as if he'd caught me being naughty. Which, to be honest, he had.

He reached over and snatched my tankard before I could do anything to stop him. He took a sip and his eyes widened in surprise.

"You're a wizard?" he asked, quietly.

"No," I admitted. "I know a few minor magics. I don't use them often."

"Just when you want to improve the flavor of your ale."

"I...can you blame me? What they serve here isn't exactly..."

"*Fen dah* of a risk just to improve a drink, isn't it? They'd throw you out of town if they caught you. If you're lucky."

"Then let's hope they don't catch me," I said, trying to sound more confident than I did in his presence.

"Just be careful," he admonished. "But first, do mine." He slid his own tankard over toward me with a big grin. "You're right about the ale in this place."

I laughed then and repeated the process. It was a small spell. The hole it poked in the veil separating our world from the other was akin to a pinprick. The danger was negligible, and the damage to the veil would be healed before we finished our drinks. The danger of being caught doing it was of greater concern.

"Oh! About time." he said, drawing my attention to the entrance of the inn, where a woman had just walked in. From her face and dress, she looked like one of the Shar'i'nol, and had a tattoo I recognized, circling her eye, marking her as a village protector, the closest they had to a warrior caste.

"What would a Shar'i'nol warrior be doing here?" I asked him.

"Just watch," he replied. "You're going to want to see this."

Two
An Unexpected Guest

THE WOMAN WHO HAD entered the inn was wearing a leather jerkin and shirt. Her sandals were laced up her leg into shin guards. On each forearm was a leather bracer to which was attached a strange knife with two curved blades mounted opposite each other into a hilt that might have been carved bone.

The jerkin and skirt combination was similar to what I had seen on soldiers in the south, where the climate was warmer than here. The knives looked like they'd be as dangerous to the wielder as to the enemy.

She spared a glance our way, nodded when her eyes met Yagmar's, but then headed toward the bar at the back of the room.

Two men who had been sitting at a table near the entrance stood up after she passed them and followed her. One of them nodded to another pair of men across the room who likewise stood and moved toward the bar.

I looked to Yagmar, but his attention was on the woman, and I couldn't tell if he even saw her followers.

They were too far away to hear, but all four men were closing in on her when she received two tankards from the bartender. The two from the front door stood to either side of her. Without taking my eyes off of them, I reached for my crwth. Yagmar saw what I was doing and shook his head slightly and held up one finger. I held off, still worried about the other two closing in, one of whom I noticed had a dagger in his boot.

One of the men who was already at the bar laid a hand on the woman's shoulder.

She shrugged it off.

He reached again, she spun and slammed her flagon into his face, knocking him backward. Her foot kicked out and swept his leg out from under him, sending him to the floor.

The other threw a punch, which she ducked while taking a long swig of her tankard. He tried an uppercut, and she brought the pewter vessel down hard on his up-rushing fist. She jumped backward as he cried out in pain and clenched his hand with his other. She spared a quick kick to one she'd knocked down earlier, as he tried to rise to his feet.

She took another step, so she was no longer between them and in one long motion, emptied her drink, turned, and flung the empty vessel toward the face of one of the two additional men who had almost reached her.

He tried to dodge, but it still hit hard enough to bloody his nose.

She spared a quick glance our way, but when Yagmar didn't move to help, turned her whole attention back to her attackers.

With a howl of rage, the man she'd just hit with her tankard leapt forward. She turned, and with both hands, helped him on the way he was already going, slamming him forward into another table.

Drinks were scattered as he slid across it and tumbled into a heap on the floor. The patrons at the table leapt angrily to their feet and I again reached for my instrument, but again Yagmar stopped me with an upraised hand.

In response to my querulous look, he said, "Just watch," and turned his attention back to the melee.

The group from the table were closing in on the man who'd been thrown across it, and he pulled a long dagger from his boot and held it in front him, keeping them at bay. I could do something about that, at least try to ensure nobody got hurt, but was following Yagmar's lead.

The woman had only two attackers left.

I still had no idea who she was or why these men were attacking her. Yagmar obviously knew something but wasn't telling.

The woman ducked another clumsy swing from one of her assailants, spun around and came up, under his arm, twisting it around and dropping him to the floor. She followed him down, still holding his arm at wrist and elbow. There was a gasp from the crowd around her and when she stood back up her erstwhile assailant did not.

The last of her attackers approached tentatively, with a dagger in his hand, extended in front of himself. I'd already seen enough to know that wasn't going to work. She stepped forward, turning and stepping to the side just as he thrust forward with his weapon.

She took his arm and turned, stepping behind him. As she did so, she brought the man's arm down and threw him forward.

There was another loud gasp from the crowd.

She stepped back into the clear and I could see her assailant lying on the ground, screaming in pain, his own dagger embedded deeply in his thigh.

Her attackers dealt with, she flipped the bartender a coin then calmly picked up her second tankard and walked toward our table.

Nobody got in her way.

The bartender called a few other people to deal with the ones who couldn't walk out on their own. I decided to assume they were taking the wounded one to a healer and spent no more thought on him while our new arrival approached.

Yagmar leapt enthusiastically to his feet as she approached. "Niala! Come, meet Oghni!"

I stood as well and offered my hand in greeting.

She looked at me but didn't take my hand. "And what's your part in all this?"

I looked back at Yagmar, who just gave me a big grin.

I turned to Niala. "Okay," I started, "What's going on here?"

"That's what I'd like to know," Niala said, glaring at Yagmar. I would hate to have been the object of that glare. "You call me here, saying there's a job, and I get jumped by four men I've never seen before while you and your friend just sit back and watch?"

I wanted to know as well. I looked to Yagmar for an explanation.

"It was an audition," he said.

Three

A Late Addition

"Audition? One of them had a knife. I could have been killed."

I tried, but failed, to stifle a laugh.

She turned toward me. "You think that's funny?"

"I..." I started, not sure what I was going to say. "Maybe a little. You were amazing. I don't think those men stood a chance."

"There, see?" Yagmar said, "Like I said, an audition. And it looks like you passed."

"Wait... what?" I stammered, and it sounded to me like Niala said exactly the same thing at the same time.

The big man turned to me. "You invited me here because you had a job, right? When I found out Niala was in town, I invited her."

"And the men who attacked me?" Niala scowled at him.

Yagmar just grinned. "It's possible that some money may have been stolen from them, and it's possible that they may have received an anonymous tip about who stole it."

She just glared at him.

Ignoring her, Yagmar turned to me. "I wanted you to see what she could do." He turned back to Niala. "I didn't know if he'd hire you just on my word—"

"How could anyone not take the word of the mighty Yagmar the Barbarian?" Niala asked as she took a seat on the bench near me. I tried not to look flustered by her proximity.

"Oh, don't you start that Barbarian *tuyot* again," he said.

She didn't respond, but instead turned to me. "What's the job? And how long will it be? I'm very busy."

"No, you're not," Yagmar said.

"Before we discuss that," I interjected before they could get started again, "I'm not sure we have more room. There's already five of us."

"And Niala will make six," Yagmar said.

"I only see three," Niala said at the same time.

"There's one more coming, and we're meeting Veldi and a friend of hers in the morning."

"Great," Niala said, finishing her ale and standing to get the serving girl's attention for another. "Is that why Yag's got his map out already?"

"I just thought it would be good to know where we're going," Yagmar growled at her. Then he turned to me, "Speaking of which. When you thought she was in trouble, you went for your instrument."

I had been hoping he hadn't noticed that.

I wasn't prepared to explain why, but Yagmar surprised me and asked, "You know Warsong?"

"Yes!" I exclaimed. "I mean, no. I mean...sort of."

"Great answer," Niala said. "Completely clears it up." She turned to Yagmar. "And this kid's going to be our leader?"

"I'm not!" I squeaked. "And I'm not. A kid, I mean. This winter will be my twenty-first."

They both looked at me skeptically.

"And I'm not the leader, either. That's Veldi. We'll meet her tomorrow. She's arranging passage."

"Wait," Yagmar said. "You're spinning us in circles. Go back to warsong. How do you know it?"

"How do *you*?" I asked. "Aside from my late mentor, I didn't know of anyone who thought it was real, let alone would assume that's what I was doing."

"I've seen it in use before. Thought the last master of it died over a century ago, though."

"You've seen it? Is it true what they say about you, then? That you're immortal?"

"Nah, not immortal. My people tend to live a long time, though. If we don't get ourselves killed. I've been kicking around for a few hundred years."

"Nakora's Eyes, I would love to know what you saw of it!"

"'Fraid I can't tell you much. I'm curious how you came to learn it."

"What's warsong?" Niala asked again.

"I didn't learn it, exactly," I answered Yagmar. Then, to Niala, "It's an old magical art, some think mythical, of controlling armies on a battlefield."

"Sounds like some powerful magic," she said. "But what does that have to do with you?"

"My mentor, Ilby, told me about it, and we'd been trying to derive some principles, seeing how much we can re-create."

"You're a wizard?" She seemed impressed.

"No," I admitted. "I was hoping to be. I'm just a singer who's had less than a season of magical training before my mentor was killed."

"But you were reaching for your crwth for the fight," Yagmar said.

"Like I said, we were working on figuring it out. I don't really know warsong, but I figured out how to do some of its effects on a small scale. I can slow someone down, distract them, or maybe make them think their enemy is somewhere else for a second."

Yagmar looked thoughtful for a moment. "I never much cared for warsong. It might win battles, but it takes a horrible toll on the soldiers. What you're describing could actually be better. A moment of distraction in a one-on-one fight could be the difference between life and death."

I tried as hard as I could to suppress my excitement at this praise. I just hoped, when it came to it, I wouldn't let him down.

"We'll have to practice with it while we travel," Yagmar said. "I don't want you throwing off my swing, and an opponent suddenly changing his timing in the middle of a fight could do more harm than good if I was counting on his sword reaching a certain place at a certain time."

"Of course," I said, still trying not to seem too eager that he had apparently already decided to join us.

"Excellent," Niala said, and I wasn't sure if she was being sarcastic or not. "We can spar as we travel, and our friend can play us beautiful music while we do!"

I was about to tell her that it wasn't up to me whether to hire her or not. I was supposed to convince Yagmar and a wizard and my instructions made no mention of finding anyone else.

"Excuse me," a voice behind me said, as if on cue. "Is one of you named Oghni?"

Niala and Yagmar both immediately turned and pointed at me.

I turned to see a youth, who I guessed had seen the harvest sixteen times at the most. He had brown skin like my own and black hair that hung almost to his shoulders and was dressed in a durable looking black robe. He wore a cloak held shut with a brooch carrying a strange asymmetrical design.

"I am he," I said to him. "Who are you?"

"I'm Taika," he said, and held out his hand in greeting.

"You can't be," I replied, and meant it. Taika was supposed to be an accomplished wizard.

"I am!" he said. He didn't say anything after that, nor did he move to sit down. If he was a spy, he wasn't very good at it.

"Who sent you?" I asked.

"Lord Embersun," he immediately replied. "He told me you were taking an expedition East and looking for a wizard."

I started and glanced around to make sure nobody had heard. Between Niala's display a few minutes ago and Yagmar's mere presence, everybody seemed to be doing their best to avoid noticing our table even existed. Still, I lowered my voice.

"Both of those things are true," I replied. "Aren't you a little young to be a wizard?"

"I went to the Academy of Pendwy."

"What?" Yagmar interrupted. "How does a wizard from the Academy end up here?"

I wondered that myself. I had heard so many stories of the splendors of the Free City. Ilby had promised to take me there some day, but of course that was never going to happen now.

"What can you do?" I asked the boy.

"For one, I can tell when magic has been used recently, and I can tell someone ensorcelled both of your drinks. But not yours," he said, turning to Niala.

If he was expecting a big reaction, he was disappointed.

"Can you tell what was done to them?" I asked him, pushing my tankard toward him.

He took a seat on the bench next to me and looked intently at it.

"It's..." The boy started, then reached out to touch the vessel. "It has! It's been chilled!"

"Shh! Not so loud!" I said. "They don't allow magic here."

"There's more, though. It looks like an illusion. Somebody covered the taste..." He looked up at me, then back at the tankard. "*Taravakan oshir*," he said, and moved his fingers through a quick gesture.

I couldn't see fast enough to determine what he was doing.

"There's no poison," he confirmed, "Or none that I can detect. But why would someone magically alter the flavor of an ale..."

"Give me that," Niala said, and swiped my tankard. She lifted it to her lips and took a large swig.

"Wait! Don't—" Taika started.

"You've been holding out on me," Niala accused, at Yagmar.

"Don't look at me," he replied with a big grin. "It was the kid's doing."

She looked accusingly at Taika.

"No, the other one," Yagmar said.

"You?" Taika said, looking at me. "Why? *How?*"

"I know a little bit of magic," I said. "I'm afraid you've seen most of my repertoire right there."

"I can answer why," Niala said. "Have you tasted the swill in this place? Oh, I am going to enjoy traveling with you, Oghni."

In the rush of feelings of praise, and relief, I mostly heard Niala saying she was going to enjoy our time together and I'm not sure if my heart stopped at that point or if it was just going too fast to register as individual beats.

Four

A Ring of Power

"So, Kid. Oghni," Yagmar boomed, shaking me out of my reverie. "This is everyone who's meeting here tonight, right? You gonna tell us what we're doing now?"

"My employer—" was as far as I got before Taika interrupted.

"Veldi?"

"Yes, that's her."

I was about to start again when he said, "And I know you're Oghni..." he started, then looked at the others.

"Of course," I said, trying to tamp down my annoyance. "Let me introduce Yagmar—"

The kid's eyes grew wide. "Yagmar the Barbarian?"

"No," Yagmar said. "That's another guy. I'm Yagmar the second night guard from the North Gate of Pendwy."

"Oh!" Taika looked confused. Perhaps he was just trying to remember if he'd ever been through the North Gate and who the guards at the time were.

"And I'm Niala," our unplanned addition introduced herself. "I don't have a title, and my hometown didn't have any gates."

"Great. Now that that's out of the way, how about the story?" Yagmar asked.

"Very well. My employer, a woman by the name of Veldi, has found..." I paused and then emphasized for effect, "The location of the lost tomb of Rhogna the Conqueror!"

For a moment there was no reaction. Taika looked confused. Niala just looked blankly at me.

Yagmar on the other hand leaned back and gave a great belly laugh that shook the table.

Half the inn must have looked over at us then.

"What's so funny?" I asked, which made him laugh even more.

"Myths of lost treasure? That's why you gathered us here? To entertain us with children's stories?"

"It's no mere story," I said. "It's real. Oh, certainly it's been exaggerated and dressed up over the years—"

"You'd know something about that!" Niala said to Yagmar, and he scowled in reply.

"But Rhogna existed," I said as if I hadn't been interrupted again. "He came from the east, past the great desert, where they say grows a forest with trees wider than this inn. And he conquered everything from there to here, and even sacked Pendwy itself. But there's no need for us to go that far. His tomb is in the mountains, and Veldi has a map and a key."

"And what makes you think this map or key is real?" He asked.

I pulled out the ring with a flourish. I'd been carrying it with me for just this purpose. I set it on the table in front of Taika. "Care to take a look?"

He looked a little nervous, then took it, and slid it onto the middle finger of his left hand. Stretching his hand in front of him he intoned, "*Taravakan Klendsha*". The ring glowed briefly with a pale greenish light. It seemed to glow brighter as he stared at it.

I plucked a couple of strings on my crwth and used the sound from them to bring up my veilsight.

The kid was working carefully. I could see the wards he wove into his simple spell, keeping the mage eaters at bay while he followed the magical connections in the ring to wherever they went.

He'd already gone farther along them than I was able to do in the time I had studied it before.

"It's definitely a magical item," he said finally. "It's got a spell in it, but it's not complete. Oh! I see... hold on," he held his other hand to forestall any questions. I knew he couldn't see us anyway. His sight was in the other world, where this ring kept its power. "It requires a wizard to operate, to remove a barrier of some sort. Yes... Oh, clever, clever. And not just any wizard," he passed his other hand over the ring and the glow immediately went out. "The user has to know what they're doing."

"And do you?" Yagmar asked him.

"Do I what?" he asked.

"Know what you're doing?" Yagmar roared at him.

Taika almost jumped out of his skin.

"Oh! No! No, it requires additional secret knowledge that only the maker would know."

There was silence around the table. I couldn't think of any response. If the ring was useless to us... if we couldn't get in, there was no point going. No glorious quest. No ancient treasure. No new song of adventure.

"Can you find out?" Niala finally asked.

"I... I don't know. Surely Veldi would know, wouldn't she? She wouldn't have gone to all this trouble without knowing that?"

I had no answer for that.

"I don't know. She's not a wizard," I shrugged. "You're probably right."

I held out my hand for the ring.

"Maybe I should keep it for a while?" Taika asked. "So I can study it? Or, since I'm the only one who can use it..."

I kept my hand out. "It belongs to my employer," I told him. "And, as you can imagine, it's very precious to her."

Five

In Search of the Unknown

Taika slipped the ring off his finger and placed it in my palm. I slid it into my pocket.

Niala turned to me. "This job that Yagmar is trying to recruit me into is... what, exactly? You want a guard while you loot this ancient tomb?"

"Pretty much, yeah."

"What's it pay?"

"I can probably get you an equal share of whatever we find." I was fairly certain I could, especially if Veldi saw her fight. "There'll be eight total: three for Veldi since she arranged everything and to reimburse expenses. Two for Yagmar, and one each for the rest of us. We can probably make that nine, and cut you in for an equal share."

"Why's he get two?" Niala asked.

I spread my hands palm up and gave a shrug. "Because he's Yagmar the Barbarian."

Yagmar gave another roar of laughter at that.

"I want what he's getting, and I'm in."

"I'm not even positive I can convince Veldi to give you one share, let alone two."

"Do we even know if there's going to be any treasure?" Taika asked. "This tomb could be looted a dozen times over by now."

"Veldi is convinced it's intact. It's magically sealed, and you have just seen the only key."

"I'm not so sure about this whole endeavor..." Yagmar started.

"Fine, you can have half of his," I decided. "Equal shares for everyone. Done, now..."

"Hey, now!" Yagmar said, and, seeing the look in his eyes, I wasn't so sure about the wisdom of my hasty proclamation.

"It doesn't matter what I say," I hastily backpedaled. "Veldi has the final decision. You can both talk to her tomorrow."

"We still don't even know if there will be any treasure at all," Taika repeated.

Niala nodded to him, then turned to me. "You're telling us we're arguing over how big of a share of nothing we'll be getting?"

"Or possibly how much of more than we can possibly carry out anyway," I replied. I didn't want to lose them at this point.

"A trek to a tomb that we might not ever find, and we might not be able to get into if we do, and there might not be anything in it if we can?" Niala summed up. "All right, I'm in." Which is not how I was expecting her to end that.

"Three things first, then," Yagmar said. "Most importantly, my tankard is empty again and requires filling, and that serving girl hasn't been over here since…"

"Since I joined you after beating up a bunch of locals?" Niala said. "And whose fault is that?"

"Fault's not the issue. My empty tankard is—"

He didn't get any further than that. Niala leapt to her feet, plucked one of the axes off his belt before he had time to stop her, and threw it across the inn, where it stuck into the wall next to the bartender, who looked stunned to see it suddenly appear.

She yelled over at him, "Dav! Get the barbarian in the corner another drink, quick!" Which earned her another scowl from Yagmar.

The bartender likewise scowled at her, but quickly poured two more tankards, and motioned to one of the servers.

"You're in charge of getting that back for me," Yagmar told her. Then he turned to me and said, "What can you tell us about this Veldi person?"

"I think she used to be a knight or something—" I began.

"You think?" Niala interrupted. "You don't know?"

"I just met her a few days ago…"

"You just joined this group a few days ago, and they made you the front for it? And you agreed? Do they even have the money?"

"Truth is, I have no idea. I was performing here, she approached me during a break, we talked a bit, and she hired me on. She'd heard you were in town and asked me to see about the possibility of recruiting you. She said it was the type of thing that might interest you."

"You musta made a *fen dah* of an impression on her," Niala said.

I shrugged. "I suspect we were both somewhat on the desperate side."

"And you trust her?" Yagmar asked.

"You saw the ring," I said, nodding toward Taika.

He shrugged. "It opens something, and it's definitely powerful."

"Good enough for now." Yagmar gestured to his map, still unrolled on the table between us. "Show me where we're going."

"Assuming we are," Niala said.

"Oh, we all know we're going," Yagmar said. "Anything else is just hammering out the details."

I had been starting to worry, so was relieved to hear him say it.

"Veldi's in port now, procuring a boat and supplies for the first part of the trip," I said, and pointed to Tenn where it was marked on the map. "From here, it'll be a nice easy journey up the Caber, to K'Gir."

I looked longingly at the map. The Caber continued past the town of K'Gir, and all the way up to Piell Under the Falls in the east. Someday, I longed to travel up there and see that city. Perhaps even more than Pendwy, Piell was known for its splendors.

"There, we'll buy mounts and a wagon, and travel the Old Trade Road, following the Tlaxam river for the better part of a fortnight. We don't know what kind of supplies we'll be able to get along the way, so we'll be purchasing everything we need in K'Gir."

"What about Tuluth?" Yagmar asked, pointing to where it was marked on the map, at the foothills to the Yikal Mountains.

"Can't be sure there will be any supplies to be had, or even if the town is still there. There's been bandit activity along the road and caravans have been lost."

He looked up. "Are there bounties?" he asked with a broad smile.

"Probably from local towns. We're supposed to steer clear of the army, though."

"Got it," he replied, and looked over at Niala, who responded with a sly smile.

"We're going over the mountains?" Taika asked, alarmed, pointing at the old road through an ancient pass.

"No," I said, and pointed to an unmarked spot. "We're going up to here, a village called Ravens Feast—"

"That's a pleasant sounding name!" Yagmar said.

"I've been there," Niala said, to my surprise. "It's the first Western village one comes to when crossing the pass. Small town, mining and fishing mostly. Nothing much special. Crossroads was a lot more fun."

"From Ravens Feast," I continued, "We cut south, through a secret pass, and travel about two more days to get to the site of the tomb."

"Kind of out of the way," Yagmar said.

I smiled at that and quoted what Veldi had said to me. "If you want to keep a tomb secret, you don't build it next to a highway."

"What's the third thing?" Taika asked, looking to Yagmar.

"What third thing?"

"You said there were three things? Your ale, where we're going, and...?"

Yagmar thought for a moment then finally said, "Ah! Yes! The songs!" He looked at me. "You said you traced the original song of Rhogna the conqueror."

"Yes?" I said.

"Stage is empty. Let's hear 'em!" He tossed a silver coin up onto the platform at the end of the large common room and, I didn't need any more encouragement than that. I climbed up onto the stage with my crwth and started my performance of the evening.

A Rude Awakening

I woke to a pounding in my head.

It took me a moment to realize there was an equally loud pounding at my door.

It had been a late night, singing, drinking, and talking. I'd gone through my entire repertoire of songs regarding Rhogna the Conqueror, and many others beyond. People in the crowd, not just my table, tossed coins all around me and kept buying me drinks. The songs grew raucous, then bawdy, and eventually slow and melancholy.

It was a good night. I smiled at the memory as I stood up and searched the floor for my trousers. I glanced back to my empty bed. It could have been better. I shrugged and got dressed before stumbling over to the door and flinging it open.

Taika stood out there, hand in mid swing.

"What?" I bellowed at him. His shrinking away was revenge enough for my pounding head.

"They... uh...they told me to come get you right away. We have to leave now."

"What? Who? Why?"

"She...Veldi...arranged a ship, and it's all loaded, but the captain said she's not waiting any longer. We have to go now."

"You mean right now?"

"Yes! Right now! Come!" With that, he grabbed my pack and crwth both and ran out the door. I had no choice but to grab what I could of my remaining clothes and follow him in haste, stumblingly putting on my boots as I went.

I caught up to him in the street and bellowed "Stop!" when I was right behind him.

He stopped, and turned toward me, his face ashen. I took the pack from him, and hastily stuffed the rest of my clothes into it, along with the knife that customarily hung from my belt. The crwth, I hung over my shoulder by its strap.

Taika sprinted away as soon as he saw I was done.

I hastily followed him through the narrow streets of Tenn.

He ran through an alley, and when we came out, the docks lay below us. Taika ran down the steep street toward one of the ships, yelling something I couldn't hear.

The crew of the ship were already casting off. They couldn't be serious. How could they leave without us? This wasn't the coast. They weren't dependent on the tide here. I redoubled my speed.

By the time I got there, they'd already pulled up the gangplank.

Taika leapt easily across the small gap and landed nimbly on the deck before he turned back to face me. The others in our group were standing beside him, watching me sprint toward the departing ship.

Yagmar was laughing as I ran while Niala was cheering me on.

Taika just looked bemused but was standing by as if waiting to help. At least, that's what I hoped he was doing.

The ship was moving parallel to the dock, and I ran along it, dodging the workers there. I flung my crwth across the gap and Yagmar caught it as I'd hoped he would. If it had fallen into the water there'd be hell to pay for this little stunt. I sprinted the rest of the way up the dock and leapt across the widening gap.

I slammed into the side of the ship, desperately grabbing for a handhold, and felt several hands upon me, lifting me up to the deck.

I turned, furious, to see who had done this, and was face to face with Veldi. She was standing, in her armor, with her customary metal shield on her back and sword at her side. She shook her head slightly at my glare.

"What's the idea?" I demanded. "You couldn't wait two more minutes?"

"I had already waited two more hours than I had agreed to," a woman I didn't recognize standing next to Veldi spoke. "I was not of a mind to wait a second more."

"Two hours? Why didn't someone tell me?" I asked her.

"I sent Taika," she said, still fixing me with that glare. "And I told you yesterday we would be leaving this morning."

"Yes, but..." I looked up. The sun was high overhead, shining brightly enough to make me immediately wish I hadn't. I had been counting on a bath this morning, followed by a nice leisurely breakfast. Apparently, that was not to be. There was nothing for it now.

"I hadn't realized it was so late," I told her. "My apologies."

She gave a curt nod. "At least you made it."

Niala, behind me with Yagmar, said, "Yes. He did."

I turned, and she had her hand out toward Yagmar, palm up.

"Aright, you win," Yagmar grumbled as he pulled out a small bag of coins and placed it in her hand. It immediately disappeared into her cloak.

Before I could say anything, Veldi spoke continued. "This is Captain Geyith. She's agreed to take us as far as K'Gir. Stay out of the way of the crew, and you can find a place to stow your gear and unroll your bedroll at night. You did bring one, right?"

Aside from the previous two nights, it'd been two fortnights since I'd last slept in a bed, so of course I had a roll as part of my pack. Given the haste of my departure, it was a good thing I'd never gotten around to unpacking.

"Captain," I nodded in greeting.

She gave a brief grunt and a nod of her head in return, which I took as an apology for my troubles as well as acceptance of my apology for making them wait. Maybe she didn't see it that way, but if she wasn't going to press the matter, I certainly wasn't.

"And this is Lonto, the fourth member of our group." Veldi introduced a tall broad-shouldered man who was now approaching us.

He wore a heavy cloak but no obvious weapons. He held out his hand to me. I took it, trying to ignore the disdainful expression on his face. Standing there with boots unlaced and doublet unfastened, perhaps wasn't a great first impression.

After they wandered off, Niala led me over to a spot of the deck that nobody else seemed to be using, and Yagmar handed me my crwth back.

"You bet against me making it?" I asked him.

He just shrugged sheepishly.

"If you knew it was a possibility, why didn't you wake me earlier?"

"Then I wouldn't have won twenty crowns."

Seven

An Unfortunate Encounter

"Twenty..." I started, then trailed off. The pouch he'd handed her must have been filled with gold. I'd never seen that much money in one place in my life.

"You didn't win twenty crowns," I realized.

"Nope. But I won't hold it against you. You can buy me a drink next time we see a tavern, to make up for it."

I laughed. "Good enough. Thanks for catching my crwth. I wouldn't want it damaged."

Once I'd secured it to the side of the ship alongside my pack, I tried to see what I could do to help out the crew. Veldi had paid for our passage, but I figured it never hurt to ease someone else's work some small amount. Although I was no sailor, I could stand in one place and hold a line, or pull it the direction I was told, or coil a rope once I'd been shown how. I was surprised how much work there was, constantly, even on such a small ship. By the third day, they'd grown to trust me enough to let me take my turn on the crow's nest, watching for pirates, among other hazards.

"How can I tell if someone's a pirate without them attacking us?" I asked.

"Watch to see if they change course to follow us," I was told.

Twice I called down possible ships, and twice we subtly changed course and the ships moved on as they were going. They were both false alarms, but nobody chastised me over it, so I guessed I was doing something right.

Yagmar and Niala were sitting on the deck with their backs against the bulwark when I climbed down the rope ladder attached to the mast. I walked over and joined them, taking a seat on a convenient barrel.

Niala held a small stone in her hand, painted with some abstract designs. She looked at it in contemplation. Beside her on the deck was an unrolled leather container with brushes and several small clay jars. She removed the stopper from one of them, dipped a brush in a mug of water, then the jar, and applied a brilliant blue pigment in a line, turning the stone as she drew.

She muttered something softly in a language I didn't recognize.

I was about to ask her about the stone when Yagmar did it for me. "What's that one going to be, then?"

She looked up and seemed to notice me for the first time. She thought for a second, then, her voiced pitched low so only we could here, said, "This one's for reincarnation. The subject will be reborn into our world and gain another lifetime."

She said it so casually, but I could barely contain my excitement as I did my best to keep my voice quiet. "A soul stone? You're creating a soul stone?"

She nodded.

"Among her many other talents," Yagmar said, "Niala's a high priestess of Arakthala."

"Does that mean that if one of us dies, you can bring us back?" I asked her.

"Afraid not. There can be only one resurrection stone in existence, and I don't have it. I don't know who does."

"Were you raised in the temple, then?" I asked. "Is that where you learned to fight?"

"No," she said. "I had teachers as a child, but a lot of it is self-taught. My religious instruction was separate. I think that's enough for today." She dropped the stone into a leather pouch at her side, then placed the stopper back in the paint jar and rolled it up with brushes.

"Where's everybody else?" I asked.

"Belowdecks," Niala said. "Taika's pouting because Veldi won't let him do any magic."

"While you sit up on deck and..."

"As far as anyone knows, it's just a painted rock. You and Yagmar are the only ones who know what they really are and I'd like to keep it that way."

I nodded. "Of course."

"Taika said he could help with the wind, and she forbade him from mentioning that to the captain. The big guy—"

"Lonto?" I asked. I assumed she wasn't talking about Yagmar, who was sitting right beside her.

"Yeah, him. He seems to only come out at night. So, he's probably hiding in the hold somewhere. Our fearless leader—"

"Veldi?" I again prompted. I felt some loyalty to her after all, as without her I wouldn't be here.

Niala just nodded this time. "Conferring with the captain, no doubt. The two of them have been spending a lot of time together."

"I think they're old friends," I said. "I don't know if the captain knows what we're up to, though, so I wouldn't go talking about it."

"Thanks. I never thought to keep a secret mission quiet before," Niala said.

Yagmar just rolled his eyes.

"Sorry," I said. Of course they were both more experienced at this sort of thing than I was. "You've been to Pendwy?" I asked Yagmar, changing the subject back to a something he'd mentioned a few days ago.

"Yeah. A few times. You would definitely like it there."

"And he really was a secondary night guard on the North Gate," Niala said, with a slight laugh.

"There's an amusing story there?" I asked. "I wanna hear it!"

"Not until you're much older," Yagmar said.

"If you don't tell me, I'll make something up."

He just laughed. "I look forward to hearing what you come up with!" Off my skeptical look, he continued. "Most of the stories I hear about me never happened, what's one more?"

I gave up, "For now," I reminded him, and picked up my crwth.

For the next few days, I played frequently on the deck. The crew would join in singing, and they had taught me some very bawdy sailor's songs to add to my repertoire. I promised to play one of them "the next time I'm at the palace", to the uproarious amusement of everyone there.

Occasionally, I wove some subtle directions into my music and set it amongst the sails to give us just a little more headway and make everything just a little easier to manage. If the captain or Veldi suspected what I was doing, though, they kept it to themselves.

Taika never showed any petulance at me stepping on his toes in such a way, though he did see what I was doing and gave me a sort of knowing smile and a nod.

It was on the fifth day up the river that we ran into trouble.

I was sitting with my back to the side of the ship, watching Yagmar and Niala gambling with some of the crew. I had decided I'd lost enough for the day and was just relaxing as they played. There was a scattering of copper coins with a few silver mixed in between them in three unequal piles. I thought of the small bag of gold coins that Niala had hidden on her person right now. The money in the pot was nothing to either of them but yet they both seemed fully invested in the game.

Niala had just thrown the dice when the call came.

"Ship incoming!" The man in the crow's nest shouted down. A moment later, "They're flying the banner of King Ta'an!"

I relaxed, but Yagmar turned to me and said, quietly, "Pick up your instrument. Stand ready."

I noticed the sailors seemed on edge as well. Many of them stood back from the game. One quickly lifted the corners on the three cloths the piles of coins were sitting on, transforming them neatly into bags, which he stowed near my pack. Another moved over to the side of the ship, and just happened to stop near where one of the crossbows was secured a couple of paces from me. He gave me a reassuring smile, which did not make me feel reassured.

The other ship quickly caught up to us, and a gangplank was lowered.

I couldn't hear what was being said to the captain by the woman who had crossed the gangplank, until our captain finally said, loud enough for us all to hear, "Over my dead body!"

The emissary from the other ship drew his sword and lifted it as our crew sprang into action. A hail of crossbow bolts flew from the other ship toward where our captain stood. I thought she was dead for sure, and the rest of us soon to follow.

Deciding I had nothing to lose, I raised the bow to my crwth.

Eight

Blood in the Water

I called my own style battlesong, though I wouldn't admit that to most people. I was trying to replicate an art that had been dead for over a century. Ilby had encouraged my endeavors, though I'm not sure he believed it would ever bear fruit. Even he had never seen it practiced, and only knew about it from other people who had heard about it from others.

Also, I had never actually used it in a real fight before. Until this moment, it had been purely theoretical, and I wasn't sure if maybe I might be of more use with a crossbow.

That decision was taken away from me as I realized all the crossbows hanging around the ship had been claimed.

So, it was either my crwth, or leap forward with dagger bared to immediately die on the end of a soldier's sword. That seemed likely to be my fate soon enough, there was no point rushing it.

As the hail of crossbow bolts reached the top of their arc. I assumed anyone near the bow of our little ship was dead, but then a great wind blew upward from the river.

Water sprayed everyone on both boats as the missiles were carried harmlessly away, and I looked around for Taika as I could only think this must be his doing.

He was crouched behind a crate lashed to the deck, peeking out, mumbling to himself, and concentrating for all he was worth.

Taking a cue from him, I ducked behind as much cover as I could while still able to see our enemy. I drew my bow across the strings and began rippling the veil around me. I had nowhere near Taika's knowledge or expertise to tear into the veil itself, but I had a few tricks of my own.

A dozen soldiers, all in armor, were starting across the plank, and more planks were being lowered.

I changed my tune—literally—and wrapped the ripples in the veil around the lead soldier, letting him feel the song, move to it, guide him toward the edge of our boat and then, right as he was nearing the end, changed the tempo ever so slightly.

The planks were already wet from Taika's deluge. I took advantage of it. A minuscule delay and slight upward change in one note were all it took to get him to step where I wanted, slide his boot off the plank and fall backwards into the fellow behind him. They both fell into the water below.

Yagmar saw his opening and took it, as I had hoped he would. He sprang forward, axe upraised, and brought it down hard on the plank itself. It splintered and fell away, and half a dozen armored soldiers fell with it, sinking out of sight.

A wall of wind and water was still spraying upward between the ships. A volley of bolts from our own crossbows met the wall and likewise flew upward. The kid obviously didn't have the fine control needed to let them through.

Our captain barked some orders I didn't understand, but we began moving. The wall of wind slid behind us then stopped. More crossbow bolts flew across the deck, and a bolt took the man next to me in the chest.

Niala swung over, snatched up the dead man's crossbow, loaded it, and launched a bolt, nearly all in one motion. A man on the other ship fell to his death.

I again ran the bow along my instrument's strings, searching for a target. I spotted Yagmar, his axe slung again from his back as the enemy had moved off. He loaded a crossbow and as he aimed it, I played a tune to match the rocking of the ship, steadying his aim. He loosed his bolt, and another enemy soldier fell back.

He smiled broadly as he loaded another.

I heard a great cry from the enemy ship and looked to see a sail smoldering for a second before bursting into flame.

My late mentor, Ilby, had taught me how to see the veil separating our world from others. I was doing so already, so I could see how my ripples were affecting it. Several rips floated around both our boat and the enemy's. Taika was pulling a lot of energy through the veil to cast the fire as he did, and I could see, dimly, the spirits on the other side moving to stop him.

He could see them as well as I, if not better, so I didn't bother with a warning, but I was concerned about how close they were getting. He'd have to stop using magic soon or wait until our ship had moved further away.

We had managed to put some distance between our ships, but I was beginning to doubt that that was the best choice.

Ours was a merchant ship, designed to carry large amounts of cargo quickly up and down the Great River.

The other, a war ship, was designed only for destruction. They seemed intent on demonstrating this, as they uncovered a pair of great ballistae that would have been at home on the turret of a castle.

Nine

Up the Creek

At the same time the crew was aiming the ballistae, another was scrambling to put out the fire on the sails. I had an idea.

Leaving Yagmar to aim his crossbow on his own for a bit, I sent another ripple across the veil. I found an enemy soldier who looked like he was in charge. I changed his perception - it wasn't much, but it was enough. He barked an order at one of the crew operating the ballista. After a brief moment of arguing, the other man complied, raised the ballista, and sent a missile high over our heads.

When it went by, it looked like a pair of baskets with a chain connecting them. Whatever it was, it sank into the river behind us.

We continued to gain distance away from the enemy ship.

I tried to do the same trick for the next ballista while the first one was being reloaded, overcompensating with the aim to make it fall short. This one learned his lesson too quickly, though. When the soldier argued with him, he let him have his way, and the chain between the twin baskets launched at us caught on our mast, swinging the baskets around. When they crashed into the deck, they spilled out a noxious smelling oil which immediately burst into flame. I leapt back and out of the way of the crew, who sprang into action with buckets, filling them with water to pour over the flames.

A great wave arose from the side of our ship and crashed over the deck, washing away the burning oil with it, and I knew I'd made the right choice to simply get out of the way. There was cursing from some of the sailors who'd been doused themselves, but I knew they'd get over it.

There was no denying we had a wizard among us now, though. Some of the crew looked toward me, playing my crwth during the battle. Hopefully, they'd decide it was all my doing and any ire would be directed toward me, not Taika. With any luck, they'd get over any prejudice they had against magic once we'd saved their ship.

I turned back to the ballistae, both of which were loaded and being cranked again. I could slow down the cranking, maybe even confuse the captain into firing into his own ship. Which gave me an idea.

This would be the most dangerous of the magic I'd worked so far, and the mage eaters were gathering all around. I drew the bow across the strings again, rapidly, while concentrating on a spot ahead of me and just to the left where there was already a weak spot in reality. I teased it open and pushed my will through it.

I could sense the angry spirits on the other side and knew I didn't have much time. I pushed through that world and into another I knew connected to it. Reaching out with my will, shaped by the music I was playing, I quickly weaved a conduit, from myself, to two worlds away, and back into our own a hundred paces away.

The effects were not subtle. A basket, being loaded onto a ballista, instead smashed downward at the feet of the soldier loading it. From there, the oil spread, then burst into flame, catching the ballista with it.

The soldiers immediately called for buckets, and the first one to the water was hit by a crossbow fired from our side.

Before the angry spirits could reach me, I slammed the conduit closed.

Then I turned my attention to the other ballista, which again launched before I could react. Its load flew toward us, then soared into the air, then turned back toward the enemy ship. I heard a cry of pain behind me and Taika fell to the deck.

There'd been too much magic thrown about. He'd cast several spells and I hadn't helped with that last one.

Seeing him fallen, Lonto stepped out from behind the cabin where he'd been hiding. He took two great steps and leapt off the ship, toward the enemy. He was still wearing his heavy cloak as he plunged headfirst into the water. I looked around, and saw Niala loading her crossbow, and Veldi nearby doing the same. Yagmar was helping Taika to his feet. At least half the crew was down. We had to take out that ship. I turned to look to see what I could do. The second ballista was loaded again. They cranked it around and fired. I had nowhere near Taika's power. There was nothing I could do to deflect it.

I reached again into the same world. The spirits were gathered, though, and I could feel them closing in on me before I could even start the weave. I snatched my hand back and again slammed shut the barrier, hoping to catch one of them between worlds, purely from spite. It wouldn't do any good. There were always more where they came from.

That path closed to me, I tried to think of something else when the baskets hit and the air around me burst into flame.

I was engulfed and with half a second to act, and only one way out of the fire, I dove headfirst into the river.

Ten

On Stranger Shores

I let the momentum from my dive carry me under the water then swam under the surface for as long as I could hold my breath.

I undid the clasp of my cloak and let it fall behind me into the river. It would only drag me down. My crwth I kept slung on my back. It would also slow me, but I couldn't stand the thought of losing it. I hoped the brief exposure to the water wouldn't do too much damage.

When my lungs could bear the lack of air no longer, I pushed to the surface and burst up out of the water. For a moment it was all I could do to gasp in the air. I looked for the ship and hoped somebody would be able to toss me a line.

The fire was even worse than I'd thought. The entire deck was ablaze. The ship was lost. A large number of people were in the water, most of them closer to the ship than I was after my panicked swim underwater.

The enemy ship, victorious in the battle, had extinguished their own fires and was lowering boats, presumably to take on survivors. Saved from drowning only to hang later.

I looked toward the shore. It was a long swim, but if I had been well-rested and not being pursued, I probably could have made it. Unfortunately, neither of those were true.

As I began to despair, the biggest fish I had ever seen leapt from the water right in front of me. In its mouth it had caught a long rope, and a piece of broken deck was attached to it. Veldi lay on the wooden board, grasping the other end of the rope.

"Grab hold," she said, reaching for me as she went by. I took her arm, and she pulled me onto the board with her.

"The others?" I shouted.

"Just hold on," she shouted back, so I did, as tightly as I could, while we were pulled at great speed through the water, by some giant fish that was inexplicably heading toward the far bank.

When we were close, the fish slowed, then turned, and started back the other way, rope, board, and all.

Veldi and I both stumbled to the shore. At this point, it was shallow enough to walk. I got the impression that our fish friend somehow knew that. For a second, I watched it go, trying to puzzle it out.

Far out into the river, I could see our ship still ablaze. It wouldn't last long. Soon, it would join all the other ships that had sunk in this river over the millennium since it was first formed. Whatever treasure was still on it might someday be found and resurface, years or decades from now, in some market in Tenn, or Pendwy.

I could see the board we'd come across as it made its way across the river, the fish somewhere ahead of it, underwater.

As I stood on the shore watching in amazement, it stopped for a moment and a figure climbed onto it. It went further, disappeared into smoke and it was several anxious minutes later that we stood peering out over the water before we saw it again. Two more figures had joined the first.

The wooden plank with its cargo of three grew closer, and eventually I could make them out. Niala was easiest, as she was standing near the front, holding the rope as if she were driving a chariot. Yagmar sat behind her, holding what must have been Taika, who wasn't moving.

This time, when the great fish reached the shore, it leapt out of the water to land on the shore right next to us. Before it hit the ground, it transformed, and there stood Lonto, still in his heavy cloak and carrying his staff in one hand. He looked like he might have just been out for a stroll. He stood watching while Veldi and I helped the others struggle to shore.

Yagmar was carrying Taika, but when they reached the shore, Taika demanded to be put down.

"I can walk!" he said petulantly.

Yagmar set him gently on his feet and he took one step then fell face-first to the ground, with a muffled cry that sounded something like "Mrifk.". A few seconds later, after catching his breath, he said in a small voice, "It appears I was wrong."

"Were you hit?" Veldi asked him.

I hurried over to him. "Was it mage eaters?" I asked, remembering his cry of pain as he cast his last spell on the ship.

He nodded, facing me as Yagmar lifted him up again.

I reached for my crwth and strummed the strings, producing a sound to carry the spell I was attempting.

"No!" Taika said. "No magic!"

"It's all right," I reassured him. "I'm only touching the nearest veil, just enough to see." Even with the malevolent spirits of the next world gathered around, attracted by the use of magic, something as simple as the veilsight I was using should be safe enough. Especially compared to the magic we'd both cast recently.

"They hit your bone," I told him. "A good part of your shin is gone. I can fix it, but not here, we need to get away. Half a league at least."

Taika just nodded in understanding.

"You can fix a broken shin with magic?" Niala asked.

"It's not broken, it's gone," I said, rather than lose esteem in her eyes with the real answer. "Malevolent spirits from beyond the veil. They always attack and devour magic users from the inside."

"Is that why wizards always look like that?"

I knew what she meant. "Partially. Any wizard who uses too much magic eventually has parts eaten away and replaced several times over. It's bound to leave some scars."

"And that's what you wanted to be?"

"It doesn't have to be like that," I objected. "If you're careful, and avoid fights, especially the military—"

"Speaking of both those things," Veldi interrupted. "We should move away from here," Veldi said. "There'll be soldiers combing these banks for survivors soon and we don't want to be found anywhere near. Can you walk?"

"I... I don't think so," Taika replied. "I'm sorry."

"You have to be half a league away to fix him?" Yagmar asked me. I nodded.

"I can carry him," He bent and lifted the boy effortlessly. "Let's go."

Eleven

A Dream of Dragons

For hours we trudged through the thick woods, enduring the cold and constant dripping of rainwater from the trees. The sun was low on the horizon by the time we stopped, near the base of a small, uplifted rock shelf. We'd seen no sign of the soldiers. Veldi said they wouldn't want to stray too far from the river, or from a road, of which we'd seen no sign.

With the cliff to one side providing a convenient wall, it looked like a good place to camp. Veldi gave us our orders: She, Yagmar and Niala would gather firewood while Lonto found us something to eat. I was to attend to Taika. All the provisions we'd picked up in Tenn were now at the bottom of the river, along with my pack containing everything I wasn't currently wearing.

"I'm perfectly capable of hunting for our dinner," Yagmar protested.

"So's Lonto," Veldi replied, "And he's better at it. You can get more wood than he can. Don't argue. I'm freezing, and I want a fire."

He nodded and headed out into the woods.

Lonto likewise walked out to the edge of the woods, but as he got there, changed shape again and a sleek black cat slinked off into the underbrush. A handy ability that, and I could see why she put him in charge of hunting.

"Won't the soldiers be likely to see that?" I asked Yagmar, when he got the fire going.

"Bring them on," he grumbled. "I didn't get a chance to use my axe on any of them on the ship."

"But it's not likely to be seen far," Veldi said, emerging from the treeline carrying several large branches. "These woods will swallow up the light pretty fast, and anyone out this way is more likely to be crew than soldiers. Regardless, we'll set a watch."

I was feeling better after a hot meal and some time by the fire.

Taika was feeling better after I knit his shin back together. It was a painful process, but it was over in a matter of minutes. It was also about the most advanced magic I knew, involving reaching through three different worlds. The mage eaters were already beginning to gather by the time I was finished.

I let Taika light the fire once it was set up. That was a trick that I'd learned from my late mentor the first time I'd been hit by mage eaters. Some wizards, especially early in their careers, would shy away from magic after such an injury and even if they do continue to pursue the craft become so reticent and full of self-doubt that they never become good at it.

I also had a trick to distract them. It wasn't quite as powerful as the wards that I was never very good at, but one thing I did figure out how to do was to sort of "ripple" the veil by playing music a certain way. I could set up a pair of these ripples and have them create a tear in the veil at a distance away from me. The mage eaters would be drawn to it and ignore the magical working nearby. It didn't always work, and never for more than a minute or so, but that was more than enough time for Taika to start a fire.

When the fire was going well, I let the small tear I'd made seal itself. Let the spirits howl their anger on their side. Spirits can't work magic, and unless some fool wizard tears open the veil between our worlds, they can do nothing to us.

The sun had well set by the time dinner was ready. It was crude, but filling, fare: strips of meat roasted over the fire.

"What about the creatures that live around here?" Taika asked as we were eating.

"What about them?" Veldi responded.

"Won't they be drawn to the fire?"

I just smiled. The kid had obviously not spent much time outside of cities.

"It'll deter more predators than it would attract," Veldi responded. "Even if it wouldn't, though...well, it's probably going to be a cold and miserable night, and there's no point making it more so by foregoing a fire."

"I'm more worried about finding water," Yagmar said. "We'll need to do that soon, we're just about out."

We had only a few waterskins between us. Mine was attached to my pack, currently at the bottom of the Caber River.

"I can do something about that," Taika said. "If you don't object?"

Veldi looked to me.

I shrugged. "Should be safe enough if it's not a major spell," I said.

"Go ahead, then," Veldi told him. "Be careful, though. I don't want you injuring yourself anymore. You've already more than proven your capabilities, you don't need to put yourself in danger."

Any farmer can tell you that the plants around us, the trees, the soil, and even the air itself contained water. The spell was simply a matter of moving it from where it was, distributed all around us, to where he wanted it to be, concentrated in our water skins.

I watched him work the spell, determined to learn how to do it myself. I wanted to get a full day's travel, at least, behind us before I risked practicing with it myself, though.

Veldi assigned Yagmar and me to the first watch. The best and worst fighters together, I guessed.

I settled in near the fire but facing away from it so I could see without spoiling my night vision.

Yagmar did the same nearby.

"So, kid, what are you going to do with your share of the treasure?" He asked me as the others settled in to sleep.

I hadn't even thought about the treasure or our mission. I realized I was thinking of our adventure as being over, with the ship sunk and in our current situation, lost in the wilderness.

Which I realized was exactly the kind of thought Yagmar was trying to fight against by asking the question the way he did, where the others could hear.

Realizing what he was doing, I decided to help him.

"I want to travel," I said. "Maybe put together a troupe of entertainers, get a whole caravan and travel the old festival route for a while. I want to see Pendwy, visit the Dancing Dragon Inn, maybe buy a house nearby where I can spend winters and eventually retire to."

"Think city living would agree with you? I thought you were a farm boy."

"I grew up on a farm. But it never agreed with me, either. I was hoping a real city might."

"There's something to be said for it, especially Pendwy, I'll give you that. Maybe I'll come visit you some day."

"What about you? What will you do with your share? Or is that shares?"

"Hah! Niala bit that in the bud. Careful entering any negotiations with her, you'll end up owing her everything in the end."

"I can hear everything you're saying from ten feet away, you know," Niala's voice came from behind us.

"Yeah, well, that's why you never discuss what you're being paid with the others on your team," he said.

"No, that's why you should always discuss it," Niala retorted. "Keeping quiet about it only benefits your employer."

"I'm right here too," Veldi said, and I allowed myself a smile. "Now keep it down, some of us need to sleep."

"I still want to travel," Yagmar said, a little more quietly. "I haven't seen everything yet. After this, I might make my way east, across the desert. I've always wanted to see a dragon."

"I told you there's no dragons east of the desert," Niala said.

"You didn't go far enough. What's on the other side of the great forest?"

"Not dragons."

"Sleep!" Veldi commanded.

Yagmar smiled to me, though. Mission accomplished. The others were thinking about the future again, and assumptions had shifted to finishing the mission. I wished them pleasant dreams of great wealth and luxuries.

Twelve

Ere Break of Day

The night passed without incident. I drifted miserably between half-waking and uneasy sleep full of disturbing dreams that I couldn't remember. Finally, for the first time in my life, I was happy to wake with the dawn.

The sky was clear, which just made it colder below. At least it wasn't raining.

"We don't know that Tuluth is even there still, let alone has enough supplies!" Veldi said, as I blinked my eyes open the next morning. She and Yagmar were sitting around his map, which was unrolled on the ground.

"If their supply chain has been raided by bandits, then we can find the bandits and take what we need from them instead," Yagmar replied.

Niala was watching impassively, sitting on a nearby log, painting a rock. At least some of her supplies had survived. I got up and wandered over. I noticed Taika was still asleep. Lonto was nowhere to be seen.

"It's too risky," Veldi repeated.

"It's a shorter trek through these woods. We'll save days from our overall journey."

"Unless there's nothing there, in which case we'll add twice as many days to it."

"Not if we can at least get mounts, or join a caravan going to K'gir."

"There won't be any caravans. The entire Tlaxam is cut off until...until the king can get his armies up there to clear out the bandits."

I wondered what she was going to say there. Why would all travel up the river be suspended? I didn't say anything, though. I'd had a sneaking suspicion that there was more to this than met the eye and her hesitation, though possibly innocent, was another mark in that direction.

"Worst case scenario, we add three days to our journey, and all of it along a road, instead of trudging through this miserable forest," Yagmar said. "But in the best case, we save four days and skip the entire roadway from Tuluth to K'gir, which is where the bandits are most likely to be located anyway."

"I'll think about it," she said, then turned to me. "What do you think, Oghni?"

That wasn't the question that interested me at the moment, though. "I want to know why the king's soldiers attacked us on the boat, and why you're so eager to avoid them still. Surely they don't make a habit of hunting down and killing every shipwreck survivor."

"We killed a number of them before they moved off."

"Even so, it seems unlikely they'd comb the woods just to catch a few random stragglers who were no threat to them."

She hesitated, and saw that both Yagmar and Niala were eyeing her with interest.

"I suppose you have a right to know," she finally conceded. "This map and key? I didn't just find them. I stole them. Rather, my partner did."

"Stole them from who?" Yagmar asked.

I had a suspicion I knew the answer, and she confirmed it.

"They were in the royal library. Naheela found them while researching something else. Ta'an didn't even know he had them, they were just stuck in some old books that he found on his travels, brought back, and added to his library without ever even reading them."

"How'd she even get access?" I asked, and it was not for purely academic purposes.

"She had family connections. Even so, it took her nearly a year to finesse them to the point where she was allowed access to the royal library. When she found out what the key and map were for, she took them out of the library, and passed them on to me. Unfortunately, they had some kind of spells that would detect when anything is stolen from the palace."

That didn't surprise me, and it might be useful knowledge later. If not to me, I might be able to sell it to the right people. At the very least, I could gain prestige by dropping the fact in conversation at the right time and place.

"How'd they track them down to you, though?"

"I don't know. I know she gave them my name before they killed her, and the king knows whose tomb it is, so now he wants the treasure for himself."

"Because that's what the man with more wealth than anyone in six kingdoms needs," Niala said. "More of it."

"What were you planning on doing with the treasure once you found it?" Yagmar asked her. It was the same question he'd asked me last night, though the context was different now.

"I want to use it to move Naheela's daughters out of Marisanti before Ta'an finds them, and use the money to raise them myself, far from the monarch who tortured their mother to death."

"What about revenge?"

"Against a king? I'm a merchant. I wouldn't even know where to begin."

Yagmar nodded, apparently satisfied. There was something else there that I was missing. Why would he care if she wanted revenge against the king or not? Nothing about that had to involve him.

I found myself thinking about it, though. I could come up with a dozen scenarios, each more improbable than the last, how a merchant might take revenge on a king. I wasn't going to say anything out loud, of course.

Thirteen

A Dance in Darkness

In the end, Yagmar won out.

We finished the meat from the night before and began our cold trek eastward through the forest.

Lonto again barely spoke throughout the day, beyond "There is water over there," or "Turn north for a bit. Large predators to the south." He proved an able guide, finding animal trails that led the direction we wanted to go, and discovering springs and, in the evening, another rock shelter to camp at. He spent half the day as an animal himself, which I found fascinating, but he rebuffed all my efforts to discuss it until I stopped asking out of fear of angering him.

On the second night, Veldi assigned us to the same teams, and the same watch order. I took the opportunity to try to learn more about Yagmar's past. I was curious which of the many stories I knew about him were true. Or, even more interestingly, which weren't. If I could learn the real story behind any of the legends, those could become very popular songs indeed.

I was mid-sentence when he suddenly held up a hand. "Quiet!" he hissed. "Don't move."

I froze, not daring to even reach for my knife or crwth. I assumed he wouldn't bark an order like that at me unless there was a *fend dah* of a good reason.

There was a noise in the underbrush behind me.

"Down!" he shouted, and I fell to the ground, turning in time to see a great creature, as long as I was tall, leap out of the underbrush directly at me. It was covered in sleek black fur and had six legs that I could see clearly as it flew through the air where I'd been standing and fell to the ground right next to where I lay now. I quickly rolled away from it and sprung to my feet and gaped in astonishment. There was an axe embedded deeply in its face, between the eyes.

I turned to look back at Yagmar who held the axe's twin in his hand and was scanning the forest past us. I hadn't even seen him throw.

I looked back out into the woods.

"Are there more?" I heard a voice behind me.

I jumped and Veldi was standing there, her sword in hand.

I hadn't heard her approach. I glanced back over to the rest. The only one I saw was Taiko, who wasn't moving.

I didn't see where Niala and Lonto had disappeared to.

For a moment, I hoped the thing Yagmar had just killed wasn't Lonto.

"Probably," Yagmar responded, quietly. "Atotho usually hunt in packs."

Atotho. I'd heard of them. Powerful and stealthy, they could outrun a horse, swim, and climb trees. Specimens had been found twice as long as a grown man is tall, and there were rumors some reached twice that size.

I carefully moved to the dead one and pulled the axe out of its forehead. It was a beautiful creature and I felt sad it was dead. I handed the axe back to Yagmar, who took it with a simple nod of thanks, replacing his second one in its loop.

"Here they come," Yagmar said. "Ready your crwth. Time to test your battlesong."

We had planned to practice but hadn't had a chance yet. He was staking a lot on my word. Or maybe he just assumed I'd be useless in a fight. Either way, I was determined not to let him down.

"*Krepi-esci monotivilla!*" I heard behind me. Taika was up and gestured in the same direction I was facing. Lights appeared, dimly, out of the darkness ahead of us. Hundreds of tiny lights like fireflies, flitting about, and half a dozen much larger, obscured in the underbrush. Every living creature in the forest ahead of us was emitting a dim glow. Which meant we could now see the creatures attacking us.

Yagmar let fly the axe I'd handed him before drawing his battle axe and charging forward.

I drew my bow across my crwth, interfering with the vision of his target, hoping to make it think him farther away than he was.

I have seen soldiers carrying axes, though none as large as the one Yagmar carried. I had never seen them fight with them before now. I had somehow assumed that they were used in a chopping motion, like I would do when cutting wood for fires.

That's not what Yagmar did, though. It was a dance. He stepped forward, sliding in a fluid motion, the axe itself becoming an extension of his arm. He didn't swing it so much as guide it, draw it alongside himself as he moved. I could barely tell what he was doing, but he stepped toward one of the beasts, extending the axe to his side. He turned as it passed and drew the axe back in and the atotho took only two more steps before falling to the ground.

I could see the pattern now, and what he was doing. A dancer needs music, so I set to work.

He whirled, and one by one, I encouraged the beasts to move to just the right place where they could meet his spinning axe. It struck high as a cat leapt, and swept low as he sank almost to the forest floor, taking the legs from another. There was force behind the blows, yes, but also angle, and timing, and movement, its sharp edge not chopping, but slicing through flesh and bone alike.

Fourteen

A Song and a Dance

Niala joined him in the dance, her two double-bladed daggers weaving a complex pattern as she rolled forward, under the belly of one of the great beasts to come out the other side, knives high and splattered with its blood as it thrashed on the ground.

Veldi sprung forward, sword in both hands, and thrust it deeply into another as it tried to pounce.

Its light went out.

Another of the atotho crept up behind Niala, and I played a discordant note, convincing it of a low opening that wasn't there. I joined it with a high chord while the note still hung in the air and Niala saw immediately what I was doing.

She leapt up, over the beast's jaws and planted both knives into its head, then drew them out as it passed.

While Veldi guarded the flank, Yagmar and Niala formed a wall through which no beast could pass. It was awful and horrific and deadly and stunningly beautiful.

I knew as I played that I was creating a bond between them. No magic beyond the music itself was needed. I had seen it in ballrooms and barns and village greens across the five kingdoms. A couple, joined in dance, soon to disappear together to be joined in an even deeper way. I stood back and provided the music that let it happen, giving the joining that one last catalyst that it needed. I had fallen in love and now I was sending my love into the arms of another. I wept as I played, for the beauty and perfection of it as much as for my own loss.

It was my own fault, of course. It's not mind control that I was doing, but I'd be lying if I said I had no influence.

Within minutes, nine Atotho, beautiful and graceful and deadly, lay dead at the perimeter of our camp. I sank to my knees, exhausted, and Lonto, of all people, was there to help me up and guide me back to the campfire.

I glanced back in time to see Yagmar, breathing heavily through a wide lustful grin, catching Niala's eye.

She too was breathing hard, she caught his eye, then turned away with the briefest shake of her head and followed us back to the fire.

A second later, Yagmar followed suit. My heart broke as it leapt in my chest, and I didn't know how to read any of this.

The wizard lights in the forest all faded out and the only light was from the campfire, and the stars shining brightly overhead.

None of us were ready to go back to sleep as Lonto put more sticks in the fire. I was still basking in the afterglow of a successful performance.

"That...that was incredible," Yagmar proclaimed. "The next inn we visit, I'm buying you the biggest drink, and of such high quality that you won't even have to magic flavor into it!" It took me a moment to realize he was talking to me.

Niala smiled at me but didn't say anything. What I wouldn't give to know where her thoughts were at that moment.

"Sorry I missed all the fun here," Lonto said to her. "I came back as soon as I heard the music. I found a better camp site, and suggest we move there. Low cliff with a waterfall into a pool. You two especially should wash up tonight, before you attract every scavenger in the forest."

Yagmar caught her eye, then a moment later turned to Lonto. "You know, those pelts can be useful, if we can process them."

"I can do it," Lonto said. "If Taika will help me."

"I'm...I'm not sure," the boy replied. "I've never done anything like that."

"I can skin and clean them, but I can't tan them here, I'll need you for that if you're up to it."

"I can try, if you can show me what to do."

"I can explain how some of it works," Veldi said, "I've tanned hides, though never with magic."

"We can go ahead to set up camp and wait for you to finish," Yagmar said.

"I'm not so sure we should split up," Veldi objected.

"It'll be safe enough," Lonto said. "Our friends here will guarantee there're no other large predators within a few leagues."

"A good idea, then," Yagmar said. "Enjoy your pelts, we'll set up camp in the new location. We should take the musician."

Veldi looked to Lonto, who shook his head. "The three of us can handle everything here."

"Be careful, then," Veldi said to me, and I stood to follow Yagmar. I gathered as much wood from the pile as I could carry.

It was as easy to find the new location as Lonto had said. We started the fire with the wood we had brought, near a fallen log we could use as a bench.

"It'll take a couple of hours for them to finish their work, even with magic," Yagmar said, "The moons are both up, which'll give me plenty of light. I'm going to gather more firewood, this isn't enough to last the night. I should be back before the others. Scream in terror if anything attacks."

I gave a short laugh at that, though if it came to it, that's exactly what I would do.

Yagmar walked into the woods and quickly disappeared from my sight.

Niala stood as soon as he was gone. "I'm going to take Lonto's advice and wash up. Will you watch?"

"Uh..." I started, surprised by the request.

"Stand watch," she clarified. "So nothing sneaks up on us. There may not be any more animal predators, but I wouldn't be certain the king's soldiers aren't still looking for us."

"Oh! Yes. I can do that."

I moved to the far side of the fire, so I could sit with my back to it, letting me have its warmth but keeping it from spoiling my night vision.

It was a beautiful moonlit night. I picked up my crwth and played a soft tune, an old song from a land as far away from my home as my home now was from me. There was a story that went with it of a sailor lost at sea and a mournful spouse awaiting his return. The melody was beautiful and sad and fit as I gazed out into the forest that seemed to stretch on in all directions onto the ends of the world.

Fifteen

Pursuit by Firelight

The sound of my crwth playing, as gentle as it was, nearly masked Niala calling my name from the pond.

I turned to see her, treading water in the middle of the pond with only her head visible above the surface.

I set my instrument on my bedroll near the fire and walked to the edge of the water.

"I don't think there's any danger," she said. "It'll be a while before anyone else is back, why don't you join me."

I didn't have to be asked twice. I stripped off my traveling garb, the first time I'd removed it in three days, and lay it on the bank next to Niala's armor, boots, and two graying bands of cloth. Her knives, I noticed, had been removed from her bracers and placed side by side on a rock right at the water's edge.

My own outfit was turning gray as well and I realized it was likely getting pretty rank. Normally, even traveling, I would have bathed and changed at least a few times by now.

I stepped into the water and gave an involuntary squeal at how cold it was. I took another step, which elicited another, smaller gasp. Niala laughed out loud at my reaction. I glared at her in mock anger then decided I might as well get it over with and dove in, not accidentally causing a great splash as I went, directed right at her face.

"Oho!" She said, "That's how it is!" and with both her hands raised a great wall of water, which I tried and failed to dodge. I shook my hair and wiped the water from my eyes with my hand. Then ran it through the water in a great slice. She may have had years of combat training, but I had four siblings and grew up by a lake. I would pit my skills in this sort of fight against anybody's.

She leapt then, landing on me with both hands on my shoulders and pushed me under the water. My brother had done the same thing to me when I was younger, but the effects of her bare chest pressing into my face were significantly different.

I went down without resisting, and kept sinking until I was below her, grabbed both ankles and yanked straight down.

She sank beneath the surface as I'd intended, but then, as I was trying to come back up, she pushed off against me, sinking me further.

I was so surprised I lost the air I was holding. I desperately kicked for the surface. When I reached it, just as I gasped for breath, I was hit by a wave of water as Niala did another two-handed splash.

I couldn't see her for a moment as I turned away, choking and coughing out the water. When I turned back, she was waiting for me, sitting in the shallow water near the shore.

She had turned and faced me with a strange smile on her face.

I acknowledged her mastery of the game and swam to her.

She leaned toward me as I approached.

The water was shallow here, and I could touch the bottom. I rose up slightly and leaned in, meeting her waiting lips. They parted softly and mine did as well.

And then, just as our lips touched, a jet of cold water shot toward the back of my throat. I pulled back in shock and got the rest of it in my face.

She'd been waiting, with a mouth full of water, for just that moment. She pushed me then as she rose and I fell back into the water, coughing and sputtering again, nearly choking I was laughing so hard.

She climbed out of the water and, picking up both her knives, walked naked to the campfire. She added more wood to it and stood, facing it, warming and drying herself.

I pulled myself out of the water, and the air seemed almost as cold now. I made my way over to the fire and stood close myself, opposite her. Her knives I now saw were arranged neatly on the log beside her.

"I'm sorry," she said, failing to stifle a laugh. "But you should have seen your face!"

"No hard feelings," I said, laughing myself. "There was no harm done, except to my ego perhaps." I sketched a big performer's bow then, "I acknowledge the game, and my better."

She did laugh out loud at that.

I stepped around the campfire toward her and reached out.

She took a step back. "Still you pursue me?" She asked. "Even after losing your game?"

"Onto the ends of the world," I said. "And I can lose a thousand games."

Her laugh was high and sweet. "Be careful my little hunter, lest prey caught prove not so sweet as that pursued."

"But how can sweetness be measured without tasting both?"

That drew another smile, but she stepped back again. "Come," she said, "We're both dry enough, and loathe as I am to put back on my dirty clothes after a clean bath, I think it's time to do so."

I nodded, withdrawing for the moment. "I was considering washing mine," I told her. "I could do yours as well if you wish."

"I don't want to wear them wet," she said, "And somehow I don't think you have any soap on you."

"I can dry them quickly," I said, " As for soap, I don't have any yet." I gave my best sly smile. "But I know where to get some."

"You've convinced me," she said, "I'll help." And the game was on again.

Sixteen

A Little Night Music

I picked up my instrument before we went back to the rocky shore where we'd left our clothes. Niala picked up her knives as soon as she stepped out of the water.

"You're never more than a few steps away from them, are you?" I asked.

"Not for many years," she replied. "It's a habit you should get into as well. If things happen quickly, like they did at the last camp site, a couple of seconds could be the difference between life and death for all of us."

When we got to our clothes, I strummed on my instrument, plucking at the strings as I pushed my will again into, and through, the veil. I knew the world I wanted, and reached it easily, accompanied by the right tune. I strummed louder for just a moment to push past the resistance.

A while back, Ilby and I stayed for almost a fortnight in a particular boarding house in a town far to the north of here. There, I had worked for the proprietor to earn our keep. And while I did that, I hid in a particular closet while practicing magic. I learned the planar boundaries around it well.

I pushed a conduit to it now, through a world that allowed such things, and let me reach through it. From one shelf, I pulled out a small white bar of soap used for washing clothes. They had several, and even if they missed one, they were unlikely to ever solve the mystery of what happened to it.

I presented it with a flourish as I caught it and ended my song. With my veilsight raised, I could see spirits moving to investigate the disruption in their world, but I ended it before any of them got too close.

"If you can do all that, can't you just magic them clean without the labor part?"

"It's possible," I confessed, "But much more difficult, and such a thing would surely draw the attention of the mage eaters, and we may end up needing magic later."

"In that case, I'll help," she said.

Together, the two of us stood, knee deep in the cold water. I scrubbed the clothes with my ill-gotten bar of soap, rubbing each item, pressing it against a rock, and pushing the detergent and water through it. When I was done with each, she rinsed it out, holding and turning it under the water, then lay each in turn on the stone of the shore. The armor, I didn't use the soap on, but merely rinsed it off, with a bit of scrubbing with my hand.

"Now how do we dry them?" she asked when we were done.

"Let's get back to the fire. Hold each item up one by one, let me see them in the light while I play."

She did so, though I noticed she started with her own small clothes and then her armor, putting each piece on as I dried it. This spell was far easier than conjuring the soap bar. Although I pierced the veil, it was to a different world than the one I usually went through, and only enough to move a significant wind, accompanied by the water, into. This was a hot, dry, and empty world, and each piece was dry within seconds.

When I was done, I also dressed, and sat on our log, facing the fire. I wished I had a cloak, and I hoped that Lonto and Taika would be successful with their work. I picked up my crwth again, contemplating what to play.

Niala sat nearby on the ground. Her knives were back in their usual place on her bracers. She took a stone from her pouch, and unrolled her painting kit on the ground. I wasn't too surprised she saved it from the shipwreck, though this is the first time I had seen it since then.

After a few minutes, she looked up from her project, past the fire, out into the nearby forest. "That song you played earlier," she asked. "Where is it from?"

"It's from Chaal," I told her. "Why?"

"It's beautiful. Full of longing, and sadness. You get the impression of someone waiting and watching, maybe looking out towards sea wondering if their lover will ever return."

"There are words that go with it," I said, "And that's exactly what they speak of. It's a common theme for songs from that region."

"Probably a common occurrence," she said.

I thought about it. How many ships had sunk, how many lovers never returned from sea, for them to have a whole collection of songs based around the theme?

"Do you know any songs of the East?" She asked. "Any of my people's music?"

"I know one," I said. "I think it is, at least. The man who taught it to me told me it was a Shar'i'nol lullaby. Would you like to hear it?"

"Please."

I played. It was a simple song, as most nursery songs are. There was something haunting about the tune that I'd always liked. A thread of hidden menace just below the surface, a promise that innocence and joy could never last.

When I finished, I set down the crwth again and found her looking straight at me.

"I know this one. I haven't heard it for a great many years. It's commonly sung to children, but it's no lullaby."

"The man who taught me said there were words that went with it, but he didn't know them."

"There are. I'm no singer, but it's one of our history songs. It speaks of a battle long ago, in our ancient homeland in a deep forest. I'm no poet, but as near as I can translate, they are *'As we frolicked in the trees and built our foolish homes, the dragons bred and grew. We knew nothing of far lands and the first we knew of danger is when the dragons arrived. And distant Shar'i'nol now lies in ruins. A land where dragons dwell and nobody builds homes in the trees.'* It's a warning against ignorance and complacency. Important lessons to all Shar'i'nol children."

"I'd love to hear them!" I said excitedly.

"Later, then. We've still got a lot of traveling ahead of us." Somehow a fortnight of walking didn't seem so bad with the prospect of Niala for company along the way.

Seventeen

An Interlude with Thoughts and Frets

I continued playing softly on my crwth, while Niala painted her stone in silence. It was such an idyllic way to spend the evening, I didn't want it to ever end.

"Of all those songs you know of Yagmar," she finally said, looking up at me when I'd paused playing. "Am I mentioned in any of them?"

"Not that I know of. At least, not by name," I tried to think. "I do know of one that mentions a 'warrior woman' he fought alongside against a horde of demons."

She laughed loudly, a great belly laugh that reminded me of Yagmar's. These two did have a lot in common.

"You'll have to sing that one later — some time when we're all together and I can mock him properly for the misrepresentation."

"How long have you known him? Have you traveled with him a lot?"

"A very long time, and yes, we've been on many adventures together. I did fight demons alongside him once, in an ancient temple under Mount Yosith. But there were only two, not a horde."

"I'd love to hear the real story some time!"

"If you're good, maybe I'll tell you eventually."

That could be taken many different ways.

"Are you and he... I mean..." I started.

She interrupted me with a laugh.

"You're so cute when you're trying to be coy," she said. "But let's be straight with each other. The answer to your question is 'sometimes'. We have in the past, when there's nobody else around and we felt like it. We're not devoted, and I think he's rather smitten with our leader this time around."

"Veldi?" I blurted out.

"Didn't you wonder about them spending so much time alone below decks on the way up the river?" She asked.

"He's supposed to be the big star of our show," I said. "I just figured they were doing important leader stuff."

"They were certainly doing something down there," she said with a laugh. "I hope I'm not misconstruing your intentions, but I think what you really want to know is if you and I have a chance, right?"

"Yes," I replied, deciding to be as up front as she was being. "Are you interested?"

"Interested, yes, but I haven't decided yet. You're not without charm, but such a relationship can play havoc on a team like ours. Veldi and Yagmar are both old troopers. I trust both of them completely. I don't know about you."

I wanted to point out that I wasn't exactly new to this. I'd traveled with a troupe before, but it wasn't really the same. We were performing, not facing life or death fights. This was all new to me.

"Haven't decided yet?" I asked, trying to keep both the disappointment and eagerness out of my voice.

"It's not the most important decision, but I won't jeopardize our mission. Can you handle an answer of maybe later or maybe never?"

"Yes," I decided. I could hold onto hope a little longer. Hopefully we'd have a chance to be alone together again. It was nothing short of miraculous that... then it hit me. This wasn't an accident.

"You talked to Yagmar about this, didn't you?"

She laughed again. "I always thought that you storyteller types were supposed to be perceptive. It took you a while to figure that out. He has more than once helped me get what I wanted. Or who."

"He has taken a long time to gather firewood," I conceded.

"I'm sure we'll have enough to stay an entire extra day or two here if we need to. I'm guessing he'll stumble noisily back into camp about five minutes before the rest of the team gets here. Just enough time for us to hastily clean up and get dressed if we needed to."

I thought of the implications of that. Had that been a possibility, or had Yagmar misconceived her intentions? If it was a possibility, had I just blown it?

I decided not to worry about that. I'd been there before, and down that path lies madness. I would take her at face value and enjoy whatever moments we had.

I was in the middle of a bawdy song about a man with seven mistresses who all meet his wife at the market one day when we heard Yagmar approaching, noisily, from the forest.

Five minutes later, the rest of our team showed up and I laughed out loud as they entered our camp site.

"Did you two work things out?" Yagmar asked. We were on watch together again. I had my crwth in my hand, thinking of

Niala's advice from earlier. I was wrapped in my new Atotho skin cloak. It was beautiful and warm, and I thought it would be a fine beginning of a new wardrobe. If I was traveling alone, it would help strike a strong figure. As it was, they marked us all as part of the same group. An organization that could afford to cloak its operatives in rare furs. We'd have to think carefully about how we were going to present ourselves, but we could do worse.

"We did," I answered. "Thank you." I trusted him to understand that I realized his part in things and was grateful for it.

All through second watch, I slept fitfully. It had grown colder that night and even with my new fur cloak, which was large enough that I could lay it on the ground, then wrap it over myself, I shivered. But that's not what kept me up. I was still unsure about this developing relationship with Niala. Not least because she was a warrior on par with Yagmar himself and, indeed, had mentioned having been intimate with him in the past.

It didn't seem to mean anything to him, other than an act between close friends, but the sheer enormity of it was frightening. I was traveling with one of the most legendary warriors of our time, and this woman, a great warrior in her own right, had been a lover of his. What would he think about me being with her now? She thought he wouldn't care, and he seemed to actively encourage it. But was that true, or could he be fooling himself? I knew from long experience how easy that is to do.

I'll admit I was a little intimidated by her. She was far beyond me in both fame and might, not to mention riches. Was it anything but sheerest audacity to consider someone like that might be interested in someone like me? Well, I decided, what if it was? You don't reach the heights of fame and glory without the audacity to try.

Every time I woke up, I saw Veldi, pacing near the edge of the forest. I occasionally saw Niala as well. She took a much more active approach to guard duty than either I or Yagmar did. She kept disappearing into the forest, presumably patrolling nearby. But once she'd left my sight, I could neither see nor hear any sign of her. No cry of birds, no rattling of the underbrush, nothing. Until a shadow detached itself from some other location, and a silhouette of Niala appeared in the firelight.

At the end of her watch, while Veldi went to awaken Lonto and Taika for their turn, Niala came to me.

"Two cloaks, and two bodies inside them, will keep us warmer, if you're willing," she said.

Of course, I was, and told her so.

I unfolded my cloak, so it lay flat on the ground, and she removed her own and laid it over me. Then, watching me the whole time, she removed her armor, arranging it neatly on the ground near us, the bracers with the knives closest of all. Dressed only in her under clothes then, she slid between the two cloaks with me.

"Is it only warmth you seek tonight, then?" I asked, with what I hoped was a suggestive smile.

"Don't fall in love, little hunter," she said, settling against me. I put my arm over her. "I'm not your muse, and I'm not your prize."

"The idea of a muse is a myth, and I could never diminish you so much." I waited just a beat before I added, "And as for 'little', I do feel the need to point out that that water was very, very cold."

She laughed, as I'd hoped, then turned slightly, and met my lips with her own, very briefly, then turned back away.

"Now sleep," she said, "Morning comes early and we've a long way ahead of us."

I did sleep, then, better than I had for several nights.

Eighteen

Traveling Songs

I awoke to the smell of cooking meat. I opened my eyes and began to stretch, then realized where I was, and that I was alone between two cloaks.

In a brief panic, I looked around, to see most of my traveling companions, including Niala, in her armor again, gathered around the campfire, over which strips of meat were being roasted on sticks.

"Here," Yagmar said, once I'd done my business and returned from the woods. He handed me a stick he'd been using to roast a large fish, already cleaned and prepped. "The kid talked some fish into joining us for breakfast." He grabbed another sharpened stick that already held a skewered fish and held it over the fire.

I caught Niala's eye. She gave me a warm smile before biting into her own.

I took the fish from Yagmar. "You've been busy," I said. "At least you didn't leave without me this time."

He laughed loudly at that.

Veldi turned to me. "We talked about it but weren't sure if we could stand the sad sight of you so desperately running to catch up," she said.

"Plus, I'm not betting with Niala anymore, so what's the point?"

"He'll come around," Niala said to the rest of us. "He always does."

At that moment, Lonto came out of the woods. "I've found a good path," he said to Veldi, ignoring everyone else. "Even so, we should hurry. There'll be rain this afternoon, and occasionally for the next few days."

"Thank you for the cloaks, then," I said, and fastened mine about me.

He just nodded his acknowledgment and picked up another stick and a prepared fish.

"Roast the rest, and we'll eat them on the road," Veldi said, and moved to follow her own advice.

Thus began the walk.

Between Lonto and Taika we had no problem foraging for what we needed along the way. I was glad to have them both with us.

With the hoods up on our cloaks, even the rain wasn't so bad, as we trudged along with our heads down. My crwth hung on a strap under my cloak with me. When the rain let up, I took it out and played a walking tune.

When I stopped, Niala called out, "Play Yagmar the Barbarian and the Goblin Princess!"

"I hate that song!" Yagmar proclaimed.

"All the more reason!" Niala cried, to laughter all around.

"I have sworn a blood oath to pull out the tongues of all who sing that song," Yagmar said and turned to me with a mock serious expression on his face. He clapped a hand on my shoulder hard. "I am sorry, my friend, but to my Barbarian people, such a vow is sacred and cannot be broken."

"I don't know that one," I said, immediately, trying, but not too hard, to keep a straight face.

"Boo!" Taika cried.

I held my crwth toward him. "Here, you play it."

"Have anything about a small band of adventurers who found a great treasure and lived happily ever after?" Veldi asked, saving us all from having to escalate our nonsense any further.

"I think I might be able to think of one or two," I said. Truthfully, of course, I knew more than a score of such songs. Most of them involved finding out the treasure wasn't what they expected, or that it was cursed.

There were a couple of a more comedic bent, though, and I decided to go with one of those. I took up my crwth and played it while I sang:

> *Prince Baelan was in a right good fix*
> *and he was fixing to despair.*
> *His father the king was getting old,*
> *and the kingdom would need an heir.*
> *Yes, the kingdom would need an heir.*

> *He could not become a king alone,*
> *for a king cannot create life*
> *A woman was needed, and for propriety's sake,*
> *that woman should be his wife*
> *The prince was in need of a wife.*

> *He announced a contest to find his new wife,*
> *and hatched a clever scheme*

Only a fighting woman would do,
to be his new warrior queen
The realm wanted a warrior queen

A wizard was vexing a village,
his criers would cry town to town
His new wife would be the one mighty woman
able to bring him down
Kill the wizard and you'll win a crown

In the realm dwelt a thief, known as Grig,
intrigued by the thought of a hoard
While the others distracted the mage,
he'd sneak in and steal the reward
He lived by his wits, not his sword

That the contest was open only
to women did not slow him down
He'd shave off his beard and do his hair,
and of course he'd buy a new gown

"Yes," Veldi said, interrupting me at this point. "Because if I was going to hunt down an evil wizard, I'd definitely want a new gown to fight in!"

"Well, you're not trying to pretend to be a woman," Niala replied.

"Ah, overcompensating." Veldi laughed.

"Ahem." I shot them each a look. They both had the grace to look properly chastised, so I continued, though I changed the last line to acknowledge her point.

> *and of course he'd buy a new gown*
> *Overcompensating with a gown*

> *As he approached the wizard's tower he saw*
> *dead monsters that lay on the ground*
> *And the bodies of those who'd gone before,*
> *and paid the ultimate cost*
> *They had played the game and they'd lost*

> *From behind him a figure dropped from*
> *the shadow with a sword raised high*
> *And a woman's voice spoke then and said*
> *make no move, but speak now or die*
> *You're a man and I want to know why*

And while he was begging, and pleading
for life, the truth finally came
And Ora just laughed at his plan and said
"The path to our goals is the same."
"Together, we can both win this game."

There were all kinds of monsters and traps
and they sneaked and they hid and they slew
Working together, they overcame all
and their trust in each other grew
After they slew their trust grew

Through two entrances they went in in hope
that they would seal the wizards doom
From two directions, one in front, one behind,
they entered the wizard's room
They snuck into the wizards room

When they reached the top of the tower,
Grig went in first, with dagger sleeved
But the man who was there cast off his mask,

and Grig saw that he had been deceived
Grig the Thief had himself been deceived.

For where stood the wizard, now stood the prince,
and he said to Grig, You have won!
On my word as the Prince, I shall marry you now,
for why should we wait for the fun?
As a prince, I don't wait for my fun.

Alas, oh my prince, you've been deceived, Grig cried.
I only sought treasure here.
And he cast off his gown and stood wearing naught
and said I can bear you no heir.
As you see, I can not bear an heir!

But the prince surprised him and said that's alright,
perhaps your partner has more,
And he turned to face Ora, behind him now,
standing near the back door
She'd been trying to sneak out the door.

I was watching, and saw that together you fought,
and succeeded where others failed.
All the rest fell one by one by the side,
where you, side by side, each prevailed!

So I'll marry you both, side by side at my side:
my lover, and my lover, a pair!
I'll have my lover and my lover and my heir!

Nineteen

And We're Walking...

Halfway through the day my feet were sore and the morning's fish a distant memory. I'd let my hood down during a brief respite from the rain when Veldi called a stop. We sat down to eat our lunch of cold fish. That night after a dinner of some small creatures that Lonto had caught several of, along with the berries we'd gathered as we walked, we took the same watch schedule. Again, at the end of her watch, Niala and I joined our cloaks to keep warm, even with the rain falling around us.

During the day, while we were walking, Niala and I weren't open about what was going on. I made it a point to spend time with everyone, deliberately avoiding paying too much exclusive attention to Niala. I was trying to avoid the unhealthy group dynamics she'd warned about.

We all talked, and joked, and laughed, and sang, as you do on a long journey. We talked of our pasts, and our plans for the future.

Taika, I learned, really was sixteen years old and had been to the Academy of Pendwy. His family had lost a great deal of money in some political maneuvering — they were minor nobles from Pendwy — and he had to leave. He sent money home, as I did, and we compared methods. I taught him how to roll coins in a piece of cloth so they don't jingle in a package, or pocket if you're trying to be quiet. He tried to show me how to do the spell he used to fill our water skins. It was a lot more complicated than it seemed and I wasn't sure how well I could do it myself.

Yagmar, for all his mysterious past, was perfectly happy to talk about it, and he and Niala filled me in on a lot of the songs I knew, where they'd come from, and what the truth behind them was. He had had a lot of legitimate adventures, but as I expected, the songs had exaggerated a great deal.

Niala teased him again about the dragons to the East of the desert. I remembered that the song she had translated for me claimed that there actually were dragons there, but I didn't want to ask her then why she kept insisting there weren't.

Niala was from a small village somewhere in the desert. Contrary to popular opinion, they weren't nomads. She was impressed that I already knew that, and that I recognized her tattoos, even though I apparently got them wrong. Village protectors weren't quite the same thing as a warrior caste. A lot of them were diplomats or scholars. When I asked which she was, she changed the subject.

Taika had read about Yagmar's people, or so he thought. When Yagmar mentioned the huge caves under the great sheets of ice, Taika laughed, and said there were no such thing.

"I grew up in them," Yagmar growled. "I'm pretty sure they existed."

"I'd read that the Orogrim lived on the edges of ice sheets, moving with them as they grew and retreated every year," Taika responded.

"That they do," Yagmar said. "But it wouldn't do to get them confused with the Theragrim — either group would take it as a grave insult to be confused with the other."

"The what?" I asked.

"Theragrim. My people. We have wizards who keep natural pockets of air open inside the ice sheets where we live. Whole cities, sprawling passageways, always changing, a thriving ecosystem, all kept alive by wizards constantly pushing back on the ice around us. We don't have the superstitious fear of magic that you do here in the South. No offense," he ended with a grin.

"I've seen it," Taika confirmed. "No offense taken."

I had as well. Even the sleight of hand tricks I'd learned in my youth were likely to enrage the ignorant.

"You think it's bad here, you should see the desert," Niala said.

"Can you imagine?" Veldi said. "One wizard splits a continent in half, kills a million people, and a thousand years later everyone's still mad about it."

I changed the subject back to Yagmar's homeland. "An entire city, wholly within the ice?" I marveled. "I would love to see it!"

"It's beautiful," Yagmar said, a faraway look in his eyes. I'd wondered how long it had been since he'd seen it.

"How is it that in all the songs I've heard of you, nobody mentions cities of ice, or even anything about your people?"

"People want to hear about battles and fights and wooing maidens. Nobody wants to hear about great cities in ice. Do you have any songs of the Therashar? A noble people who live far beneath the mountains of Riushi. They make sculptures of crystal that direct sunlight to their caves far below, casting shadows that tell stories that take a full year to see in their entirety."

"No! Is that real?"

"As far as I know. I've heard of people who claim to have traveled there to see them. Never been myself. No idea how to contact them, either. They apparently don't trade with the Riushians."

On the third day we came to a road. It ran in a straight line through the forest as far as we could see, both ways. Trees and underbrush had been cleared for a dozen paces on both sides. It was paved with stone, and split wooden logs marked both edges. There was no doubt which road this was. It could only be an old highway of the Ilrushan Empire. Nobody had built a road like this for over a thousand years.

"The question of course," Yagmar said, looking to Veldi, "Is which way to follow it?"

"Tuluth may no longer exist," Veldi said. "Let's head west. Either we're east of Tuluth, in which case we'll come to it soon if it's there, or we'll spend two, maybe three days at most and end up at K'Gir as originally planned."

"I hate the idea of walking three more days like this," Yagmar said, "Especially when we might be able to walk less than half of one."

After a moment of thought, Veldi offered a compromise. "We'll continue east for one day. If we don't come across Tuluth, or what's left of it, by nightfall, we turn back and continue until we find it, something else, or K'Gir. Agreed?"

That sounded reasonable to me, and there were nods of assent all around.

It was only a few hours later, of easy travel along the road despite the light rain, that we saw other travelers, half a dozen, all on horseback, approaching from the east.

As they neared, Veldi stepped toward them. I could see they were wearing the livery of King Ta'an. I hoped they hadn't been in communication with the ones we'd killed on the river.

Veldi stepped forward to greet their leader, but he responded by drawing his sword.

"Aha. It seems our information was right. There are bandits out this way!"

"Hold! Hold!" Veldi cried, her empty hands held up. "We are not bandits! We're—"

But she got no further as the soldiers followed their leader, drawing their weapons and spurring their horses toward us in a charge.

Twenty

A Fight on an Ancient Road

Yagmar took a step forward, partially blocking me from the soldiers' view.

Niala had somehow disappeared again. By now, I was used to this. I scanned for cover. There was a large boulder several steps ahead of me alongside the road. I decided it would be my destination.

The lead soldier, sword raised high, didn't stop as he charged straight at Veldi.

Yagmar pushed me toward the boulder I'd spied, and I needed no further encouragement. As I moved, he plucked one of his throwing axes from his belt and hurled it at the soldier.

Before it got to its destination, it flew up into the air and far off to the left, to be lost in the distant underbrush.

Yagmar gave a roar of rage and hefted his great axe.

By then, the lead soldier had caught up to Veldi. She stood, waiting for him and when he was just about to hit her, she stepped to the side, sword in both hands and brought it up to catch his down-swinging arm.

The soldier turned in his saddle and deflected her strike. Pulling slightly back then quickly thrusting forward, he would have driven his sword into her head had she not ducked the blow just in time.

He didn't get far, though. Yagmar had nearly caught up and, on the other side of the horse, swung hard with his axe. I could see it bite down into the man's leg, through it, and into the horse beneath.

For a moment I felt sorry for the great beast as it fell and began to thrash and cry.

A great bear leapt over it, charging toward the rest of the soldiers.

I assumed that must be Lonto.

He ran straight at the five horses running toward us.

No, not five. Only four were running. The man in the back hadn't moved yet or drawn his sword.

Noticing the movement of his hands and lips, I switched to veilsight and could see it, distorted and waving in front of us. The man had at least four spells up at once.

In addition to shielding them all from anything moving through the air, he was holding Taika still. There was another distortion around him that I couldn't read but assumed was some sort of ward. And another one, piercing straight through the veil, going somewhere, a tiny conduit, smaller than the one I reached through to steal a bar of soap.

I swung my crwth around in front of me on its strap and drew the bow from its sheath. I drew it across the strings, aiming a particular note, and joined it with my voice. I was trying to push aside, or at least weaken the hold he had on Taika. It didn't work, but it did draw his attention.

"The one in back's a wizard!" I yelled. "He's got Taika!"

The wizard smiled an evil smile and made a small adjustment.

Taika fell to his knees, screaming.

Bastard was killing him, and I just gave him the boy's name to help him do it.

The four on horses were holding our three warriors back.

They were holding their own but making no gains as each slash and stab on both sides was countered, and the horses rode in tight circles around them.

I felt the inside of my chest grow cold and realized their wizard was doing something to me as well. How many spells could he keep going at once? I'd never seen such power.

My fingers grew numb and I found myself unable to hold the bow. It dragged across the strings, and I fumbled then dropped it. I fell to the ground, unable to stand. Everything was starting to grow dim when the wizard suddenly cried out in agony. I was immediately released from his grasp. I picked up my bow from the ground where it lay and peeked back out from behind my boulder.

The wizard was lying on the ground in front of Niala, gaping up at her in dull surprise.

Both her knives were in her hands and there was blood staining the ground.

I guessed she had heard me.

She turned to step away from him, heading back to the main melee where the others were holding their own.

Taika painfully regained his feet.

One of the horsemen saw him and peeled away.

A bad move on his part as a great swipe from the bear's arm caught his horse across the rump, sending it sprawling and spilling its rider.

Yagmar took advantage of the momentary distraction, leaped forward with his huge axe, reversed it, and as another soldier, still on his horse swung his sword downward, he caught his wrist with the pommel and drove back up.

The soldier kept hold of his sword but as his arm rose, the axe followed. Then Yagmar spun the blade around to swing upward and into the man's unarmored armpit.

Blood spilled out from beneath his shoulder, and he pulled on his horse's reins with the other hand as he tried to ride away.

Another throwing axe caught him in the back, and he fell to the ground. His horse kept running, and I didn't blame it a bit.

I looked again at the wizard using veilsight.

He was still alive, though wouldn't be for much longer. He was still maintaining one spell: the one with the needle hole in the veil. I tried to look through it to see what he was doing, and I felt a blow to my chest, as if the wind had been knocked out of me.

I tried to gasp for breath and couldn't inhale.

I couldn't shout a warning, either, to Niala whose back was to him as she moved away.

Twenty-One
Death in the Dust

My fingers were still working. Barely. I drew my bow shakily across a single string on my crwth and sent a ripple in the veil down to the dying wizard. It wasn't a powerful spell, just enough to get his attention. A poke in the face.

Luck held, and he let out the growl I'd been hoping for as I disrupted his concentration.

Niala spun, throwing forward one of her double-bladed knives.

It took the wizard in the throat, and I felt the grip on my own loosen, then vanish.

I gasped for breath, and was about to shout a thank you across the battlefield when something grabbed hold of my wrist. I tried to turn but fell hard to the ground.

One of the soldiers, wounded perhaps on the road, was behind me. As I fell, he rose, his sword held in both hands. He raised it to plunge directly into my chest, and I had no way to escape.

The soldier's eyes grew wide and brought both hands to the side of his face, dropping the sword. He took a step backward from me, clutching his head. His mouth gaped open and fire spewed out. Clawing at his own eyes, he fell backward and thrashed desperately. Smoke escaped his head while I watched in horror. He didn't last long.

By the time I got back to the battle it was over. Yagmar and Niala were standing side by side while Lonto, back in his human form, was cradling the limp form of Taika. Veldi was lying still, her hand pressed to her side. She'd been hit, but I judged Taika was in more immediate danger.

I rushed to him and brought up my veilsight. That last spell had taken a lot from him, and the mage eaters had taken more.

The enemy wizard must have drawn their attention with all the magic he was sustaining. There was no sign they got to him, though. If he had had any wards up, they were lost now, fluttering away on the parts of the veil he'd held with his mind.

"He'll be alright," I told the rest after examining Taika. "He's asleep, and will be for a good many hours. We'll be one short for watch tonight, but by morning he should be fully recovered. How are you?" I turned my attention to Veldi.

"I...uh... well, honestly, I could use a little help."

I knelt beside her and examined the wound. It wasn't deep and didn't look like it hit anything vital, but she'd lost a lot of blood. I could seal the wound and replace the blood, but I could sense the spirits closing in, fumbling blindly around. If I did this here, they'd find me quickly.

"Taika could do this better. Can we get one of those horses? I don't think I can do enough to get you walking, but I might get you to the point where you could be carried, if someone leads the horse. I can do more once we're a league or two away."

Veldi nodded. "Do what you can without endangering yourself. I don't want to be two wizards down."

"I'm still no wizard," I said, reaching for my bow. I could stop the bleeding and make it safe to ride. She'd be anemic, but not in any danger except of passing out. Once we got far enough away from here, I'd be able to replace the blood she'd lost, as long as nobody asked where it came from.

I again used the music, slow and gentle this time, to reach out and play upon the veil, causing it to ripple and bunch where I wanted and spread where I didn't. As gently as I could, so the spirits didn't see the hole I was making in their world, I reached through it and pulled the torn parts of my employer's flesh back together.

She gritted her teeth from the pain but didn't cry out.

When I was finished, the wound was closed. "That's the best I could do quickly. We've got to get away from here before anyone uses any more magic. There's probably going to be a scar, sorry."

"Probably." She said, with a grunt of laughter. "One more scar isn't going to hurt me."

I thought of the network of scars I'd seen across Niala's body.

These people lived dangerous lives. Every one of those scars was a moment where they had evaded death. Eventually, there would come a wound that wouldn't leave a scar.

"How safe is it to linger?" Veldi asked.

"As long as nobody uses any magic, the spirits can't get to us," I told her. "The last opening died with that one," I indicated the wizard that Niala had slain. "I'm a little worried, though. He had a spell going at the end, even as he was dying. I think it was a message. It's likely someone knows what happened here."

"Can you tell what he sent?"

"No. I'm sorry. I'm not even sure that's what it was. It was just a semi-educated guess. Taika might be able to tell us more once he's awake."

"Let's hurry, then." She climbed unsteadily to her feet. Niala rushed to help hold her up.

Veldi was about to say something else but was interrupted by a low moan from one of the soldiers. She glanced sharply his way, then approached him, sword drawn. Niala stood at her side, ready to help.

I looked with the veilsight as they approached. There was nothing there.

I nodded to Niala, who had shot me a questioning look.

"What's your name, soldier," Veldi asked the man who had made the noise.

"You'll get nothing from me, traitor," the man gasped.

Veldi lowered her sword to his throat.

"I die in service to my king. I'll go on to my just reward. Will you be able to say the same, oathbreaker?"

She slid the sword forward, then back out, and the man said no more.

Twenty-Two

Secrets and Lies

"Lonto, gather up the horses," Veldi said. "Niala, Yagmar, I want you to strip the bodies, take anything valuable, throw everything else into the forest. Hopefully there'll be nothing to connect any of this to us. Oghni, help them."

We did as she said, putting her on one horse, Taika draped over another, and the food and other supplies from the soldiers on another.

I was delighted to find a skin of wine on one of the soldiers. Niala, Yagmar, and I passed around the wine while we marched. Even with Lonto and Veldi forgoing their turns, it was soon gone.

After an hour or so, I told Veldi I believed we were far enough away to risk magic again, and she called for a stop.

As we sat on a grassy slope beside the road, I checked the dressing on her wound, and found it still good. It had not reopened, as I'd feared it might.

"How did they find us?" I asked her directly. I made sure Yagmar and Niala were both nearby when I did. I was about to replace the blood she had lost. I wanted to have this conversation before I did so, though, just in case.

From her reaction to the question, I guessed that fact was not lost on her.

She looked up at me, then over to Yagmar and Niala. If it came to a fight, I was pretty sure at this point they'd both side with me.

Lonto might join her, or just stay out of it. It looked like she made the same assessment.

I didn't want it to come to a fight.

Neither did she. "They've got to be tracking me with magic," she said. "I thought maybe spies hunted me down in Tenn, but after the ship sank, spending three days in trackless wilderness should have been enough to throw anybody off the trail. But they found us within hours of reaching the road. It had to be magic." She looked at me then and asked, "Can you do anything about it?"

"I don't think so," I answered honestly. I started pulling the bow across the crwth strings, softly, lowly, then spoke calmly so as not to disturb the spell. "The real question is why. It seems like an awful lot of trouble to go through just to retrieve some stolen bauble. Don't try to sit up yet, let me finish."

I continued my spell, knitting the deeper tissue together and pulling blood from another world, dripping it into her veins to replace what she had lost. I went slowly, and moved my connections around so as to confuse the malevolent spirits who I could sense starting to move in. My spells were gentle, though, and I would be finished before they were too close.

"It's more than some bauble," Veldi answered while I worked. "It's the key to an ancient nearly legendary tomb—"

"Which would be of great interest to people like us," I interrupted. "But why would a bunch of storied treasure be worth the time of the king to find the thief before she even got to the treasure?"

She shook her head. "Perhaps he knows something about it that I don't."

Niala looked at her suspiciously. "Like what?"

"I have no idea. But if he wants it that badly, it must be worth a lot."

"Or, maybe it's enough that we just send the key back with our apologies and go on our way." Niala said.

"What? After all that, you wanna give up just because we have some competition?" Yagmar exclaimed.

"He's right," I said. "I've never once told a story that ends with 'and then they met opposition, so they quit'. I don't want to start now."

Niala smiled at that.

Veldi looked relieved. Also, better. She was in good enough condition to fight me now, if she wanted to.

"If anyone wants out, they're welcome to leave at any time," she said, getting to her feet. "Though I hope you won't. Especially you," she indicated me. "I haven't felt this good in years. Even my muscle fatigue's gone. You do good work."

"Thanks," I said, sliding my bow back into its sheath. Sensing she had said all she was going to, I changed the subject. "Assuming we even find this town, what's our story if anyone asks who we are?"

"Our caravan was hit by bandits," Veldi told the innkeeper. "About a day's walk west of here."

The town of Tuluth was still there, and there was an inn, the Staggering Toad, a large stone building which had seen much better days.

"Why would you bring a caravan out this way with only six of you?" The innkeeper asked, as he pulled tall mugs of ale for each of us. We'd already deposited Taika up in his room, and Lonto stayed to watch over his recovery. Veldi explained that Lonto was a skilled herbalist and that the kid was being kept asleep while he healed.

"There were more of us when we started," Veldi lied smoothly. "The rest of us barely survived the fight. Our wagons were lost, or else we'd have brought you more to cheer you than our meager presence."

"You didn't know about the bandits along the road?"

"We had heard that it had been so long since anyone tried it, that they'd moved south."

"Not as long as fools keep trying to come through with insufficient guards. The king needs to send his armies out and clean them up."

"We did meet one patrol on the road. I thought they'd come from here, though."

"Haven't seen any of the King's soldiers in a season at least," the innkeeper said, which was the first bit of news we'd heard since arriving in town.

I kept my face neutral. If they hadn't come from here, then they'd only been on the road looking for us. They must have been heading this way when they got news we were on the road, so they turned around and came back to find us. Which meant someone was coordinating a search. The wizard with the patrol couldn't have been the one tracking us, or they wouldn't have gone past us in the first place.

It was quite possible that Veldi had come to the same conclusion, but I resolved to bring it up when I had a chance.

They almost certainly knew that we'd killed their patrol now, as well.

"Even if they do dispatch another patrol to look for us, the closest they can be is K'Gir," Yagmar pointed out, leaning back in his chair and taking another chug of his ale. I was on my third myself. The inn had a dozen empty rooms upstairs, and we were gathered in the largest of the four we'd rented.

"They'd take at least a few days to get to us," I added, trying to sound sage.

"Unless they have forts along the road, or patrols somewhere else," Veldi said. "As they almost certainly do."

"That would be here," I suddenly realized.

Veldi looked at me.

"This place must be one of the old Imperial Inns," I explained. "Look at it. Huge courtyard for mounts, stonework, defensible..." The others continued to look blankly at me.

"You know the old Empire, Ilrushan, right?"

They nodded.

"They had a network of Imperial Inns all over, each within an easy day's march from another. King Ta'an has been reviving the tradition. Fixing up ancient buildings like this, or building brand new ones where there isn't enough left of the old ones. Inns throughout the South have been vying for royal charter. This is the only inn within a day's march, and it fits all their criteria perfectly, probably built by the Empire. Which means, if there are soldiers anywhere, they'd be stationed here."

"Which means, those soldiers were here, and our host lied to us about it," Niala finished.

Twenty-Three

A Night of Peace and Love

"We're still in danger," Veldi said. "But we can't assay the mountains unprepared. We need supplies. Cold weather gear, a cart, and I was hoping for mounts. But nobody is going to sell us anything until morning."

"Are we safe here, then? If the keeper has already sent a message..." I trailed off. We all knew the implications.

"It's likely any backup is still days away," Veldi said. "Assuming the patrol we met was really from here." She paused for a moment, then decided. "Speculation's pointless. We need supplies, and we need to be ready to flee without them, or fight if we need to. We'll need watches again tonight, though I admit I had been hoping we wouldn't."

"I'll take first," I said. "Nobody will think twice about a musician playing late or sitting by the fire after everyone else has gone."

"Damn," Yagmar said. "I was hoping to actually get some sleep before my watch."

"I'll swap with you, then," Niala said.

Veldi rolled her eyes. She knew exactly what was going on. "Fine. Remember you're supposed to be on watch, so keep your eyes on everyone else, not each other, and check outside frequently to make sure nobody's trying to set anything up."

Our watch passed uneventfully. Niala made frequent trips outside, while I played for the scattered patrons. They kept me well, but not overly, supplied with ale. It was just as well it wasn't too much, as I was on duty, albeit in a sort of undercover sort of way. I still imbibed, of course. I felt it was important to keep up appearances.

After the last of the patrons left, the innkeeper brought me a large pitcher, then retired himself.

I continued playing one last song. It was a popular love song in the north, and one of the most requested in my repertoire.

Niala entered as I finished. She had been out making another circuit outside. Without a word she walked over to me, leaned down to where I was sitting, and kissed me. It was warm and wonderful, and I never wanted it to end.

Finally, she pulled away with a smile said, "We better get back to work before the boss catches us."

"Yes. I suppose so. Once our shift's over, though..." I started.

"Yes," she finished. "Your room."

The remaining hour of our watch crawled slowly by. I sang to her while we were inside, and we held hands when walking outside. There was no sign of hidden troops or gathering bandits, and nobody disturbed us in the inn. Before going to my room, I stopped at Veldi's and knocked loudly.

I was not surprised to hear Yagmar's gruff "Go away!" in response.

I laughed out loud and moved on.

I had lit candles in my room when Niala slipped in. I hadn't even heard her approach.

She closed the door and again we kissed while we stood halfway between it and the bed. I continued the kiss and pulled off my shirt while I did so, then began unlacing her jerkin. She glanced nervously at the candles for a moment, then seemed to make a decision and assisted me.

I led her to the bed, and she lay down, stretching on the furs that covered it.

We made love, then, by candlelight. She was surprisingly gentle, and for the most part followed my lead.

The candles burned down and went out, and, eventually, we slept.

And eventually I was awakened by a knock at the door.

I glanced around and found I was alone in the room. The knock repeated.

I remembered my haste the last the last time I left an inn, when everyone nearly left without me. Given everything that had happened since, would it have been better if I'd arrived one minute later and never got on the boat at all? I thought of last night and decided it would not. I panicked for a moment thinking they were planning on doing the same thing again.

"One moment!" I yelled out, and hastily found my trousers and pulled them on.

Taika was standing at the door holding a mug of some steaming beverage.

"The rest have gone out to secure provisions," he said. "And wanted me to make sure you were up in time and ready to go by the time they came back."

"Good to see you're doing well," I told him.

"Thanks to you," he replied.

"And likewise," I said, remembering the fate of the man who had very nearly killed me on the road.

Breakfast was waiting by the time we got downstairs. If the innkeeper had noticed we'd been setting watches all night, he didn't say anything about it.

I wouldn't blame him. We were obviously a force to be reckoned with, and if he suspected we had had a run in with the king's soldiers he wouldn't want to confront us while alone.

I was impressed with how much the others had managed to gather. A wagon and a strange six-legged beast to pull it. Tents, furs, barrels for water, and enough hard tack that we wouldn't have to hunt. Veldi had somehow found a set of new armor and a shield for herself and Yagmar replaced the throwing axe he'd lost when fighting the soldiers. There were extra changes of clothes for all of us, myself included.

"Are we expecting to do a lot of climbing?" I asked when I saw the rope and other gear.

"It's possible," Veldi answered.

"Don't worry. If you fall, I'll catch you," Taika said, divining my concern.

"Can you actually do that?" I asked him. It would take a lot of energy to arrest the fall of an entire human. I knew of three ways to do it, all of which were far beyond my capabilities.

"I haven't tried yet, but in theory, it should work."

I laughed out loud. For some reason, that did make me feel a little better about it.

Twenty-Four
Raven's Feast

There was no climbing, or doing much else beyond walking, for the first part of our trek. Despite the cold, it wasn't an unenjoyable journey. The views in the mountain pass were incredible. Back home in Tengo, the mountains were far off. Here, they rose into the sky to our left while the tree-filled valley dropped away to our right.

On the third day a light snow began falling, but my new furs kept me warm. Niala forewent extra furs, wearing nothing beyond the atotho cloak over the leather armor and light undergarments she always wore.

With the amount of furs that Yagmar layered on, he truly looked like the Barbarian of the stories.

Without feeling the need to be circumspect anymore, Niala and I only pitched a single tent at night, which we shared when neither of us were on watch.

I noticed that Veldi and Yagmar did the same.

Veldi set an easy pace, and we took turns riding on the wagon throughout the journey. She rotated our watches after we left Tuluth. Yagmar preferred the last watch of the night, as it meant he only had to get up once, and after a full night's rest. I preferred first watch, even though it came as more work after a full day's travel, it meant I only had to get undressed for bed once and didn't have to get up again until after dawn. Not that our preferences meant anything. Veldi followed her own logic for how she arranged things.

While we traveled, Lonto usually roamed ahead in beast form. Sometimes he was a bear, sometimes a hawk. Once, he took the form of our large blue furry cart puller, which I learned was called a tyroth. They were bred for this purpose and were highly resistant to both heat and cold, able to regulate their own internal temperature well. It grazed as we traveled. We weren't planning on climbing so high into the mountains that there wouldn't be vegetation, so we didn't have to bring supplemental food for it.

Occasionally, I worked on a new song, playing my crwth, trying to figure out the composition. I didn't sing the words to it out loud, though. I didn't dare, not yet, but I frequently looked at Niala while I was composing, and she caught me at it.

"What is that song?" she asked me at one point, when we were alone.

I smiled at her, confirming her suspicions. "It's for you."

"It doesn't sound like a song about a great fight, or a mighty warrior."

"No," I admitted, "It's a love song."

"You think I need a love song?"

"I think you deserve a love song."

"You think the world needs another love song?"

"This one will be different. A song befitting a mighty warrior, but a love song for the ages. It will make armies falter and the gods themselves will weep to hear it!"

I may have been a little carried away.

"The gods themselves, huh?" She said with a mocking smile. "This I have to hear."

"When it's done," I said. "I'm still having some trouble with the bridge."

"Perhaps someone needs to stand and hold it against a horde of demons."

I laughed out loud at that. "Perhaps someone does."

I hadn't seen Lonto for most of the fourth day when, just as we were beginning to set up camp that night, a hawk swooped into our midst, and he resumed his human form.

"There's soldiers coming up the road," he said to Veldi.

"How far?"

"They're two days behind us and don't seem to be gaining quickly. We should be safe for now."

She nodded. "Hopefully we'll lose them when we leave the road, then. We won't linger in Ravens Feast. Replenish any supplies we can and keep going. We'll cut south after we've passed it. I'll trust you to find us a good path once we get there."

"No fire tonight, then, I take it?" I asked her.

"If we don't, they'll know we spotted them. We'll do the same as we've done before until we leave the main road. After that, we'll just have to bundle up while on watch."

On the fifth day, we came upon the village of Ravens Feast. Like Tuluth, it had seen better days. Long ago, there was steady trade from Torlindl, across the mountains, and to the desert beyond, with Niala's people, the Shar'i'nol. It had grown from a small fishing village high in the mountains into a major trade hub. Rhogna the Conqueror had put an end to that a thousand years ago. Few traders came here now, and it was once again a small fishing village, surrounded by the ruins of its glory days.

Wooden houses at the outskirts of town had all but rotted away and even the stone buildings were crumbling and empty. The few people who were out looked at us with curiosity as we made our way up the crumbling cobbled street.

We came to a once-magnificent stone building in the center of town. Two stories tall, with each upstairs room opening onto a balcony overlooking a muddy expanse which was likely once a wondrous marketplace, the first display of goods from East of the mountains, and the first place for merchants from the East to purchase goods from the West to take home. Everything would have come here. I wondered how many merchants would have stopped here and gone no further. Why would they need to when everything they wished to purchase would have been brought here?

I imagined their ghosts plying their goods, a score of colorful pavilions set up around the market. Interspersed among them would be wagons or stalls, barkers at every shop trying to entice people to examine their wares, and everyone brightly dressed in linens or silk or furs. There on the balcony would sit a bard with his retinue, finished with a successful day of performing, sipping from a mug of ale, and overlooking it all.

We passed the building, which when I got close could see was unused and shuttered, with a sign too faded to read hanging loosely by one corner. In the next strong wind, it would come down and be scavenged for somebody's fire, a sad end to one of the last remnants of a faded empire. For this had to be not only a former Imperial Inn, but the Last Imperial Inn. I had a song about a duel that took place here. The body at the end fell off the balcony and into the lake, never to be seen again. Artistic license that, unless the victim had been hit hard enough to fly a hundred paces before landing in the water.

Next to the old inn was a smaller wooden building. Obviously newer, it somehow gave off the air of being decrepit more than the actual ancient structure it sat next to. That was our destination. It was a small place, smoky, but they had fresh fish and decent ale, and we passed enough time there to not raise suspicion before we left early the next morning. Days ahead of the king's soldiers, I hoped.

The Innkeeper himself gave us an excuse for haste. With winter approaching, we'd have to hurry over the mountain to make the pass to the East before the snow closed it for the season.

He offered to let us winter at the inn. While the lake would freeze over, he assured us villagers would still be able to extract fish from it by cutting holes in the ice, so there was food all winter long, in addition to what was already laid in store. If I had been traveling myself, and not pursued by soldiers of the king, I might have taken him up on it.

But hasten we did, though not over the pass as we told him. We headed east only for a few hours. Out of sight of the village, we cut south. True to his word, Lonto found us a path to take. It looked like it may have even been a road once upon a time. I doubted anyone had traveled it since before the Goblin War, though, and maybe not since Ilrushan itself.

Once we had left the main road, Taika, under Lonto's supervision, magically cleared our tracks, and somehow moved them to the main road. Quite a trick, that. If the soldiers were following us, though, it should throw them off, at least temporarily.

Twenty-Five

Death from Above

For three days, we picked our way along the path. The road, such as it was, was far too rocky for anyone to be riding in the cart anymore. At times, it was tilted near on its side to get over a boulder.

Our tyroth never complained, though. The good beast just kept pulling the cart slowly forward, whether it was on wheels or not. The snow was halfway up to my knees and more was falling gently as we traveled it. I was worried we'd get more, but Lonto assured me that at our altitude there wouldn't be enough snow to cause issues for us.

"Our tyroth can handle any amount," he said. "And if it gets too deep, we'll just take the wheels off the cart, and it becomes a sledge."

"That's all well and good for the tyroth," I replied, "But I can't plow through waist-high snow drifts with ease."

He laughed at that. "Don't worry, singer. We'll be long out of the mountains before it comes to that. We've got at least a fortnight of mild weather left before there's risk of heavy snowfall."

"You call this mild?"

He laughed out loud again. "Ask your woman." He indicated Niala, walking through the snow wearing the same outfit she had been wearing throughout our journey.

"Not his woman!" She called back, then walked over to us. "He's right about the cold, though. This is nothing. The first time I passed over these mountains, it was so cold you could spit, and it would freeze before it hit the ground."

As we drew closer, Veldi spent more time in the evenings with Yagmar poring over their maps.

We were all searching for the landmarks, especially a point where three peaks met a shallow lake.

As we walked, a frequent topic was speculation on how much treasure there'd be, and what we'd do with it. The treasure itself was becoming more real as more of the journey was behind us than ahead of us. There was no sign of the soldiers pursuing us anymore. We seemed to have thrown them off our trail.

I was walking alongside Niala, laughing at some joke that's only funny after spending a fortnight on the road with someone.

Yagmar shouted a warning, but before I could turn to see what it was about, I felt something bite into both my shoulders, and I was lifted into the air. Confused, I saw the ground sweep away beneath me, and Niala running for the cart.

A stench of decay overwhelmed me, and the contents of my stomach threatened to escape.

Yagmar drew back and threw one of his axes and for a second I thought he meant to hit me with it. Kill me quickly to save me from whatever horror was coming. Which was nice and all, except I hadn't even figured out what was going on let alone had time to grow terrified of it.

The thrown axe struck above me, and I heard a large squawk and flurry of feathers. The largest bird-like creature I'd ever seen flew off with Yagmar's new axe deeply embedded in its chest. I had a good view of it as I plummeted toward the ground.

The creature itself was hideous. Its ragged feathers grew in irregular patches and its head seemed somehow lopsided, with one eye bigger than the other. The talons protruded from the feet at odd angles, though they were strong enough to have dug painfully into both my shoulders as it lifted me.

It disappeared as I landed on my back in a deep snow drift. Fortunately, it had decided to carry me up hill instead of down, so I didn't fall far.

"Take cover!" I heard Veldi yelling below and remembered Ilby yelling the same thing once. It seemed like a lifetime ago.

"Get under the wagon. Hide! Whatever you do, don't let them see you!" It was the last thing he ever said to me. Like a coward, I obeyed his order, and I lived while he died. Not this time.

I was a hundred or more paces away from the cart and a perilous climb downslope at that. I saw more of the large bird creatures swooping down at my friends below.

Niala hugged the side of a cart, reloading one of our two crossbows.

Veldi aimed one from the other side of the cart.

Taika was running toward a large boulder.

One of the creatures swooped down toward him, to be met with a pair of crossbow bolts.

Taika fell to the ground and the bird thing closed its misshapen talons over the empty air where he had been.

Then Yagmar was there, standing over him with his great axe held high.

One of the creatures swooped toward them and pulled away at the last second, with a bright cut across its belly. It flopped its wings for a moment, tried to circle, then began an uneven dive toward Niala and Veldi.

Veldi stood and loosed a bolt from her crossbow. It landed dead center in the great bird, which spun and plummeted, continuing along its previous course, smashing into the cart, shattering it. The creature lay still in the wreckage

Another of the things was right behind it, though, and while Veldi was hastily trying to load another bolt into her crossbow, it plucked her from the ground and flew back upward.

Lonto took a step forward, leapt into the air and became a creature similar to those attacking us. He flapped twice and with a great pitiful squawk fell to the ground, thrashing about and dissolved into mist.

I watched, horrified, until the mist again gathered and there was Lonto, lying on his back gasping for breath.

Ignoring him, Niala fired her crossbow at the beast carrying Veldi, impaling it through the head. It dropped its catch before plummeting to the ground itself.

I wished for my crwth, below us on the smashed cart. Without it, I could do nothing. I watched in horror as Veldi fell, plummeting toward the ground, then slowed, and floated, slowly back toward the road.

I glanced down to see Taika straining, facing her, his arms outstretched.

Niala approached him and tossed Yagmar the crossbow that Veldi had dropped in her rapid ascent.

Veldi and I both arrived back at the group around the same time. The last few of the bird creatures were flying off.

Everybody seemed uninjured. Even Lonto was standing now.

I found my crwth in the wreckage of the cart, mercifully undamaged, and swung it around my shoulder. From now on, it would always be with me. I should have listened to Niala earlier, and I could have helped from the snowbank I was in. Next time, we might not be so lucky.

"Don't!" Taika cried when he saw I had it in hand.

I looked sharply up at him.

"Mage eaters. I trapped one that was attacking Lonto. There're others gathered around. It'll be too dangerous to use any magic here right now."

Twenty-Six

Aftermath and Forewarning

"A mage eater was attacking me?" Lonto asked.

"You trapped one?" I said at the same time. When Lonto didn't say anything further, I continued. "I didn't even know that was possible."

"Not many people do," Taika replied with a shy grin. "I...uh... there are places in the Academy where you can learn forbidden lore. If we were staying here, I could hold the spirit until it told me its name. Then, I could use it to summon it."

"From what I've heard, that could be incredibly valuable. I'm almost tempted to ask to stay so you can get it."

Taika shook his head. "I wouldn't know how to summon it safely, and the only people I could sell the name to would be demon summoners, whose attention I don't want and who I wouldn't want to provide aid to."

"There's wisdom in that," I said. "I know a few songs where people chose otherwise, always for the greater good. It never ends well."

"And what happened to you?" Veldi asked Lonto, who I noticed was still leaning heavily on his staff.

"I'm alright now," he said. "Those things were...not natural. They were constructed."

"They bled when we cut them," Yagmar said.

"They are living creatures, but they're not born. Somebody knit them together with magic, pulled from material from beyond the veil. When I tried to copy it...it didn't turn out well for me. They're alive, inhabited by some spirit, but carelessly put together, and they're in pain. So much pain, all the time."

"Torkcha. They have to be," I said, marveling.

"Here?" Taika said. "I've heard of them, but I thought they were a myth from a distant land."

"So's Rhogna," I pointed out. To the rest, I said, "There's a story of his inner circle riding giant flying mounts: Torkcha. These must be them. They got free somehow when he died and have been living in these hills ever since."

"These are the originals, then," Lonto said. "They can't reproduce."

"I wonder how many are actually left," I said. I looked out around the mountains. There was something sad about that, "A doomed species. Long lived, in constant pain, and never any more born. Someday, they'll all be gone."

"That's for the best," Lonto said. "Killing the ones we did was a mercy."

"It's also a good sign about the existence of this tomb," Niala pointed out. "If these mythical birds are here, our mythical conqueror may be nearby, too."

I hadn't even been thinking about the possibility of the tomb not being there anymore. I had mixed feelings about doubts being raised, justified, and dispelled all at once.

"Guess you can catch me if I fall after all," I said to Taika. "That was pretty impressive."

"I'm sorry," he said, looking down. "I... before I realized what was happening, you were already down."

I hadn't considered how he didn't catch me. "I meant Veldi. Seriously. It was fast. I was back on the ground myself before I realized what was going on. I'm not hurt, so it's all good."

"I'll try to do better next time."

"You did well this time. We're all alive and uninjured, partially thanks to you."

"Yagmar could have done more if he hadn't had to peel away from the fight to protect me."

Yagmar laughed loudly. "Kid, I've been doing this sort of thing since before your granddaddy was born. Don't think you can make better tactical decisions than I can."

Taika just looked confused.

Yagmar explained. "I didn't protect you 'cause you were weak; I knew that you were our best bet at stopping those things. I figured if you didn't have to worry about defending yourself, you'd be more effective. The real question though, is what are we going to do about the wagon?"

"I don't think we have much further to go," Veldi said. "We'll have to carry some of the supplies and load the rest onto the tyroth. I'd like to get the cart off the path, though, so it's at least a little less obvious which way we went."

"No problem there," Yagmar said, and picked up a broken wheel. He swung around in a big circle and launched it far out over the forest below us, where it crashed into a tree, disappearing in a flurry of snow. While we loaded our supplies onto our pack animal, Yagmar amused himself by hurling piece after piece as far as he could, which was impressively far.

"What about the torkcha?" he asked.

"Burn them?" I suggested. Everyone but Taika looked at me in horror.

"I can't think of a better way of announcing exactly where we are," Veldi said.

"I don't know if we can avoid that. Leaving them here will do the same to anyone who comes across them, and circling carrion birds will be just as visible as a smoke column."

"Could we bury them?" Taika asked.

"It would take too long," Veldi said. "And if done improperly, they'd just get dug up and we'd be back to the scavenger problem."

"Let's toss them into the woods, then, with the wagon parts," Yagmar said. "Something dying in the woods probably happens all the time. Suspicious, maybe, but even if they do check it'll take time."

"And if they're scattered down there, there's nothing to tie them directly to us," I said.

"I like the idea of the soldiers having to waste hours climbing down to check," Veldi said. "Let's do it."

That night we found a rock shelter with more than enough room for all of us. We forwent the tents and built a fire near the entrance. It was comfortable enough, though I think I preferred the tent. With Niala and I sharing a tent, there was more than enough warmth, and definitely more privacy.

Veldi put Niala and I on watch together. It passed uneventfully, and afterward we slept snuggled together near the fire and I had dreams of being carried off by a dragon, then plummeting into darkness.

Twenty-Seven

Descent

Five days after we left Ravens Feast, nearly a fortnight after we left Tenn, a hawk flew down to us and turned into Lonto.

"I found it," he announced. "Look, you can see the peaks from here. Those three."

I looked where he gestured. Three peaks of nearly equal size stood out, closer together and smaller than they'd seemed at first.

"At their base is a small pool, fed by an underground spring, and a cave receding into the hill beyond it. I didn't explore the cave, but I have no doubt it's what we're looking for."

We arrived in the early evening, and I was surprised that the path we'd been following led straight to it. There could be no doubt about what it was, it matched exactly the picture on Veldi's map.

"Of course the path would lead here," Yagmar pointed out. "If they built some elaborate tomb up here, they'd have had to get supplies to it."

"We camp here for the night," Veldi said. "We can assay the cave in the morning when we're all rested."

While the rest of us set up camp, Yagmar and Niala went into the cave a short distance, and came back with a report that after some distance, there was a huge set of rune-inscribed stone doors that wouldn't open when they tried.

I was excited to see these doors myself. This had to be it. What else up here could have such an entrance? It only remained to be seen if Taika could open them with Veldi's ring. As eager as I was, I saw the wisdom of waiting until morning. There was no telling how deep the cave went or what dangers lay past those sealed doors.

In the morning, we sorted our supplies for our descent. We left the tents set up outside. There was no point in striking camp if we were just going to set it all back up in the same place when we got back out. We each took a bedroll, though, and a backpack with food, water, supplies, and a coil of rope. We left the tyroth tied to a long line, so it could graze. There was no telling how long we'd be gone. If we never came back, I supposed it could eventually chew through the rope to free itself.

The light from the entrance was a dim spot when we came to the door Niala and Yagmar had described.

"And now the moment of truth," Veldi said, and withdrew the ring and handed it to Taika.

For a moment, Taika looked at the ring. I strummed my crwth and used the tone to bring up my veil sight. The runes on the door all seemed alive, with thin tendrils reaching out, swaying in an unfelt breeze.

"I'm not sure," Taika finally said, a note of desperation in his voice. "I can't read the writing. I think…"

"I can," Niala said, and all eyes turned to her.

"It's Shar'i'nol. It's weird, though. It's all fragmented sentences." She pointed at a few at random, "Like this one says *his sword raised*, and then there's *they stepped forward*, and *a flock of flightless birds*."

Taika looked excited at that. "Is there one about a boat casting off with the tide?"

Niala looked and a second later said, "Yes, here. *We left with a falling tide.*"

Taika brightened, said something I didn't catch, and I could see tiny magical tendrils reaching out of the ring. He held the ring up to the phrase Niala had indicated, and the tendrils from the runes reached toward those in the ring. They intertwined together. Then he slowly pulled away, stretching the tendrils, and spoke, "*Triar-lya!*"

All the tendrils, the warping and tiny punctures through the veil, withdrew, and as they did, with a sound of stone grinding on stone, the two large doors swung open.

"This is it!" I shouted. When they turned to look to me, I said, "There can't be any doubt at all this is the tomb of Rhogna the Conqueror."

"Good job, Taika," Veldi said. "I knew you could do it!"

He just beamed, and stood, staring at the door for a moment before he remembered to hand her the ring back.

Past the doors, a corridor stretched into darkness. Veldi lit a second lantern and handed it to me.

The passage curved for a while, then ended abruptly in a deep pit.

We tied one of the lanterns to the end of a rope and lowered it down, despite Taika's protestations that he could just send a light down there faster.

"We want to conserve your magic," Veldi told him. "When it's the only thing between all of us and certain death, I don't want to be regretting squandering it doing something we could have done ourselves."

At the bottom of the pit, the floor was smooth and flat, unlike the rough stone up where we were. The walls looked like they were made from shaped stones, leading both ways away from the chasm. Somebody had put a lot of work into either bringing in those stones to build a façade, or into carving the actual walls of a natural cavern to make it look like it.

We drove a couple of spikes into the ground to secure the rope, which we also looped around a stalagmite for good measure and climbed down. With the rope and the uneven wall, it was an easy climb, even for Taika, who'd never climbed a rope before.

As I climbed, I noticed the walls were covered with more Shar'i'nol writing, very faint and hard to read in the dim light.

"What do these say?" I asked Niala, once we had all reached the bottom.

"I don't know. I don't think they say anything. It's not words, it looks like just letters repeated in random order. Oddly spaced."

"Let me look," I said when I got there.

"Will this help us?" Yagmar asked. "Do we care about what this says?"

"We do if it's directions to get to the treasure," I said.

"It's probably just proclamations extolling Rhogna's greatness, and the glory of his deeds."

"Not unless it's in some kind of code," Niala said.

"You two want to try to figure out the writing?" Veldi asked us.

"It might be important," I said. I was prepared to make my case, but she acquiesced immediately.

"All right. Short rest, everybody," she said, then immediately dropped her backpack and sat down beside it. Lonto and Yagmar did the same, while Taika came up to stand near where Niala and I were staring at the wall.

I was trying to detect some kind of pattern but could see none.

"How many letters does your alphabet have, Niala?" Taika asked, after a couple of minutes.

"Twenty-two, plus six vowel marks."

"I only see nine symbols here," he said, "And one doesn't look like the others."

Niala looked more carefully at the symbols, then pointed. "You're right. It's just the first eight characters of our alphabet." She pointed at several symbols in rapid succession, "There's rof, nof, pof, then so, tho, sho, cho, and ta. Those are followed by ma, sa, ka, and the rest, but none of them are here."

"What about this?" I pointed to the more complex symbol that Taika had said didn't match the rest.

"That's a *cowa*. It's used in holy texts for sort of a brief pause."

That matched my suspicion perfectly.

"Does the spacing mean anything to you?" I asked.

"No, we don't write them like that."

"That's what I thought," I said. "Can you go over that order again? I have an idea."

She did so, and, after a bit of repetition, I could recite the symbols in the correct order.

"What's the point of this?" She asked.

"In Pendwy, there are musicians who write music by assigning each note to a different letter. But there are only eight notes in an octave, so they only use the first eight letters of the alphabet. They have other symbols to indicate how long to hold a note, which is what I suspect the odd spacing may be about, and where the pauses are." I indicated the symbol she had called a cowa.

I arbitrarily assigned a note to the first symbol, and, assuming they were done the same way I had heard about in Pendwy, I hummed the notes, extending the ones with greater space after them. A bit of experimentation with pitch later, I drew my bow across the strings of my crwth, confident I could play it.

The music filled the chamber. The cave had some interesting acoustics to it. I would have loved to stay and experiment with them.

I played for perhaps a minute, stumbling a few times as I tried to remember which symbol was which.

There was a loud SLAM somewhere in the distance, and then the sound of stone grinding on stone.

Twenty-Eight
Melody of a Madman

I stopped immediately as everyone else jumped to their feet.

"Was that you?" Veldi asked.

"I... I don't know..." I started.

"Taika?" She turned to him and for a moment he just looked confused.

"Oh! Hold on..."

His eyes unfocused as he looked into another world.

"Yes!" He cried out. "It's rapidly vanishing, but there was something. A conduit from you to... somewhere."

"But I didn't open a conduit," I protested.

"Are you sure?" asked Veldi.

"There's more to magic than just playing the right music, or saying the right words," I told her. "There's a focusing of will, and concentrating on the properties of the world you're pushing into, and—"

"It can't be done accidentally," Taika finished for me.

"So, if you didn't do it... who did?" Veldi asked.

"Yeah, that's the question."

"I should have been watching with veilsight," Taika said. "If you try again—"

"No," Veldi interrupted him. "Let's not try any more strange magic until we have some idea of what it does."

I had to agree with the wisdom of that. I turned to Niala. "Did you recognize the music?"

"No," she said. "Why would you think I would?"

"Shar'i'nol letters, I assumed it was a Shar'i'nol tune that it encodes."

"But it's Rhogna's tomb, and he wasn't Shar'i'nol."

"Are you sure about that? Legends say he conquered the desert dwellers..."

"Right," she said. "But he came from further east."

"Further east than the Forest of Dragons?" I hadn't told anyone else what she had told me about how her people were driven out from there.

She must have realized what she had said, though, and replied with calculated uncertainty. "I... don't know. I don't know where Rhogna came from, I'm sorry. And he never conquered us. We didn't cooperate with him, either. How can you conquer a village when the whole thing, buildings and all, just dissolves away into the desert when you approach?"

"That sounds like a neat trick, and a story I'd love to hear some other time," I said.

"Sounds like the noise came from that way," Veldi said, indicating one of the passages leading away from the pit. "Let's go see what we can find before we decide what to do next."

Niala, my love, was keeping something back from me. The problem was, I couldn't tell if it was because she didn't want to tell me, or if she didn't want to say anything in front of the others.

I wanted to talk with her alone, but there was no way to do that. Until we were out of this place, there would be no alone, for any of us. By then it would be too late. Whatever she knew about what we were about to face would have been faced.

My only options were to trust her or not. I decided to trust her. The alternative was too unpalatable to contemplate.

The passage out of the small room we were in was vaulted high overhead, both sides covered in bas reliefs. Two rows of writing ran under them, carved into the stone. The top row was in the language of the Shar'i'nol and, as Veldi translated, did indeed extol the deeds of Rhogna the Conqueror.

"Not so much about his glory on the battlefield, though, and more about what a wise and benevolent ruler he was, bringing civilization to the degenerate people west of the mountains," she said.

I wondered if the words were meant to accompany music written underneath them. It might give some hint about how the music was meant to be played. I wanted to experiment with that, if Niala would sing the lyrics as I played the music, but Veldi vetoed that idea immediately.

The hallway eventually opened into a grand domed room through an arched doorway. The passage was one of three, equally spaced around the room, and the only one that wasn't filled with stone. The walls curved up and were nearly lost in shadow overhead. Three statues, as tall as any building I'd seen, stood between the doorways, their backs bent and arms held upward, as if they were holding up the ceiling.

For all I knew, they might have been.

Near the top of the dome, almost lost in the darkness at the edge of our lanterns' lights, were two great wheels, similar to the one at the stern of the ship that had born us from Tenn. They were side by side, protruding from the ceiling at an angle.

Writing covered the walls, at all levels.

Examining the doorways showed no obvious sign of how they could be opened. It looked like they were filled with a solid block of stone, but no sign of how they were moved, or even whether. Yagmar tried to push one, and even when Veldi stepped in to help him, it wouldn't budge.

"The giants," Niala said.

While I had been watching Yagmar and Veldi, Niala had been reading the inscriptions.

I turned to look at her.

"According to these inscriptions, these are three giants that Rhogna defeated," she said. "But what's interesting is their names. That one's *Shaka'rasoo*, or *Slayer of my Enemies*, that one is *T'yooshalika*, or *Lifter of Heavy Burdens*, and this one," she indicated a figure opposite one of the sealed doorways, "is named *Shadorak'u*, which translates to *Opener of the Way*."

Next to it, like the other two, were the characters that I now recognized as musical notation.

"You're thinking that playing the music for that one would open the gate." Veldi said.

"It can't hurt to try," I said.

"Of course, it can," she retorted. "Playing with strange magics that we don't know anything about?"

"The inscriptions are obviously here to guide—"

"Guide who?" Veldi interrupted.

I fell silent, not sure how to answer.

"Exactly. We don't know. Not us. Why would they go through all this trouble, building the locks, the gates, just to leave an inscription in plain sight explaining how to circumvent them?"

"It's... not exactly in plain sight," I said. "It would require the ring, and both someone with formal training in music, and someone who knew the Shar'i'nol language."

"An amazing coincidence isn't it, then, that we just happen to have both those people with us?"

Twenty-Nine
Wards and Warsong

"I…"

Veldi waited for me to say something, glaring at me.

"What else could it be? These writings are ancient. This wasn't all built after we got together!"

"If I may…" Lonto stepped forward.

Everybody stopped and looked at him.

"Oghni is right. This wasn't built for us. It is clear that, whether or not the Conqueror was Shar'i'nol, his followers, at least some of them, were. These carvings are old. I can feel the centuries in the stone. The instructions were likely put here so that his disciples, or their descendants, could continue to be able to tend to his tomb, even if much else was lost."

"So, you're saying…" I started.

"Instructions written in such a way as to direct his Shar'i'nol followers but be indecipherable to anyone else would be keeping in line with what I know of the Conqueror," Lonto confirmed.

"All right," Veldi said before I could ask him what he knew about Rhogna the Conqueror. "I don't see any other way in. Play it. Everybody else, stand ready."

Yagmar stepped forward to stand by me, his great axe in both hands. Niala moved over to Taika and drew both her knives. Lonto and Veldi positioned themselves, side by side, between us and the two sealed doors.

I began playing the notes, as best I could, written beside the stone giant that Niala had called Shadorak'u.

I was about ten seconds in when, with a great rolling sound as stone scraping against stone, it began to move.

I continued playing.

The stone giant stepped forward, the sound of it echoing through the ancient hallways.

I glanced around at my companions. They were all watching it in awe.

I continued playing.

The stone giant reached up to the ceiling and began turning one of the wheels.

From somewhere inside the walls there was a creaking sound as of some ancient mechanism protesting being forced into movement after long disuse.

Some gear turned and something fell into place with a resounding THUNK.

And as I continued playing the song described in the ancient carving, the stone giant moved to the next wheel and as it turned it, the block of stone over one of the doorways, bit by bit, began rising. As it rose, a similar block began slowly descending into the doorway we had entered through.

We could go further in, but our exit was blocked.

We crept cautiously through the doorway into another hallway. Bas reliefs lined both walls. These were battle scenes. In many of them, warriors dressed much like Niala were driving their foes before them.

I stopped before an image of a man I knew must be Rhogna. He was standing on a hillside, lifting a staff high in his hand. Two musicians were seated on either side of him, playing some kind of horn and a stringed instrument I didn't recognize. Over all three hung more of the musical inscriptions.

"This...This may be the only existing record of warsong," I said, marveling at them.

I was about to ask Taika to copy it down but decided to get a closer look first. I strummed a specific cord on my crwth and used its vibration to pull up my veilsight.

A thousand demons sprung at me.

I dropped the veilsight, and fell away from them, landing on the floor with a cry of shock.

Niala was at my side instantly.

"What's wrong?"

"I..." I started, as I tried to stand.

She assisted me to my feet, and Taika began to do something.

"No!" I shouted to him, "Don't..."

He held up a hand. "It's all right, they can't get through."

"Who can't get through?" Veldi demanded.

Yagmar had unslung his axe and was holding it in both hands, ready to move in any direction.

Lonto was his usual impassive self, quietly watching Taika.

"Mage eaters," Taika said. "Hundreds of them. Maybe thousands. They're trapped, all around us. It's like... I've never seen anything like it."

He thought for a moment. "You know how it's safe to use magic inside the Academy in Pendwy, but you can't use it at all outside the walls?"

"No," Veldi said.

Taika laughed. "Well, um, it is. It's because of the wards. Generations of wizards, the archmages, the instructors, down to the students, constantly strengthen them. Mage eaters can't get through them, so it's safe to cast within. But wards attract spirits, too. They gather outside the walls, and if anyone uses magic out there, they'll attack immediately."

"So, we just passed outside of the same type of wards?" I asked.

"No. Inside. Only, backwards. So, kind of outside, yes."

"You've lost me," I told him.

"Somebody did the same thing here, but looped them back around on themselves. It's like they cast wards, waited for the spirits to gather, then went around and finished a wall of them, trapping the spirits inside. They can't get out. They've probably been trapped in there, howling in anguish, since the tomb was built."

"And it's these angry spirits that are all around us right now?" Veldi asked, looking every which way as if she might spy them. "But you say there's no way to get to us. So, what would be the point?"

"No way they can get to us, unless someone uses magic to pierce the veil. Then they can all get to us. The least they'd do if I try to cast anything here is kill me. At worst, they'll rend the veil and come through into our world and possess or kill all of you as well."

"So effectively they've made it impossible to use magic in here," Veldi said. "Clever."

From the darkness there came the sound of stone grinding on stone.

From the reactions of the rest, I could tell they heard it too. There was movement in the shadows, and Veldi turned up her lantern and aimed it in that direction. In the lantern's light, I could see a row of stone statues come to life and marching toward us. The bas-reliefs had torn themselves from the wall and were advancing.

The ones nearby were beginning to do the same. Stone shields and spears held high, the figures stepped in unison. Contoured in the front, we could see their backs were perfectly flat.

Down the hall, more were beginning to do the same.

"Run!" Yelled Veldi, then followed her own advice.

I followed, running down the hall into distant darkness.

The creatures were closing in on us.

There was another doorway at the farthest reaches of our light. We weren't going to make it.

Thirty
Soldiers of Stone

We kept running, even though the weird flat-backed moving statues were closing in from both sides of the hallway in front of us, blocking our path.

Veldi's shield smashed into one at full force, knocking it down.

Yagmar swept his axe low into the legs of another. Sparks flew where the axe struck, and one leg was shattered beneath it. It toppled to the floor and shattered into a hundred pieces.

There were more figures getting closer.

Veldi repeated the smashing maneuver with her shield, using both hands to swing it around, opening a path for us to advance.

Yagmar stood beside her. He poked at one with his axe, pushing it backward, before flipping his weapon around and smashing the pommel into its face. It seemed a dangerous move, but I noticed there was already a chip in the sharp edge of the axe. Much more of this could destroy it completely.

If Yagmar's axe would be damaged by the stone soldiers, Niala's razor-sharp knives didn't stand a chance.

I glanced back and was surprised that somehow she had wrangled a stone club. She swung it in great sweeping arcs, taking out more of the moving statues. There were more of the things behind us than in front of us, and she and Lonto were doing their best to keep them back.

I felt useless, sandwiched between them, unable to do anything. I could tell Taika felt the same way.

Step by step we advanced toward the end of the hall.

By the time we got to the doorway, there were no more in front of us, though they pressed us still from the sides and from behind.

Taika and I ducked through it first, and the rest followed quickly behind.

"The wheel, there!" Taika said, pointing to a large spool of chain leading up to the ceiling.

I recognized the device immediately, and realized what it was for. I took hold of the mallet that was leaning against it. I picked it up and as soon as Yagmar was through the doorway, I swung the mallet to knock the locking peg out of the ratchet. The wheel spun as the chain flew up to the ceiling and a heavy portcullis slammed down in the doorway.

The gate crashed down between us and the creatures. They ran headlong into it, stone arms and weapons reaching grotesquely through the bars, writhing and grasping toward us.

For a second, I thought we were safe. Then they began lifting the gate.

Yagmar stepped forward again, placing himself between the stone creatures and the rest of us. There was another new chip in the middle of one of his axe blades.

Our weapons couldn't last forever against these things. Then I saw it: One of the creatures, with its arm stuck through the gate, was being lifted off its feet. In its hand was a mace, held loosely. I sprang forward and leapt up, stepping on the bottom cross bar as the gate raised, and grabbed the thing's wrist in both hands, pulling and twisting.

Its other hand reached forward and grasped my neck, pulling me into the crossed bars.

This wasn't going as well as I'd hoped. I continued trying to pull the mace free. Perhaps it could help Yagmar's axe, and prove I wasn't completely useless.

I got the mace free and tried to transfer it to my right hand. As I did, another hand shot out, grabbing for it. I yanked it away but lost my grip and it fell to the floor. I didn't realize how far up I'd moved with the gate. The ceiling was rapidly approaching.

There was a smashing sound next to me. Veldi had jumped up onto the gate, in her hand was the mace I'd prized from the moving bas-relief figure. Her swing shattered the stone arm that was holding me to the gate. I leapt free and she followed half a second later. She rolled to her feet when she hit the ground, swinging low to smash the feet of the figures below.

Veldi tossed her new mace to Yagmar, who caught it and immediately began swinging. She took her shield in both hands and brought it down hard on the statue's feet. They broke beneath the blow, and as the figure fell to the floor, she smashed down hard again on its neck.

Its head shattered and it lay still.

Niala leapt forward, dropping the ruined remains of her stone club. She grabbed hold of a leg of one of the moving figures and lifted it up, knocking the thing down.

"Right here," she said to Veldi, indicating a spot just above the knee.

Veldi understood what she was asking and brought the edge of her shield down hard on the indicated spot, and now Niala had a serviceable club, rounded on one side and flat on the other where it had sat against the wall. She swung it up, then down into the head of its former owner, knocking it backward. It shattered when it fell and moved no more.

The four of them held the line. I tried to step up to do my part, but Yagmar growled at me. "Stay back, protect the kid."

I decided my ego could survive being irrelevant for a few minutes. I wasn't going to mention it in the song I'd write about this battle, though. I stood behind them, with Taika, who was looking back and forth, feeling obviously as equally useless. I kept looking further down the hall, expecting something even more terrifying to emerge from the darkness, but so far nothing did.

But hold the line they did, and eventually started pressing forward.

The creatures, constructs, whatever they were, seemed endless at first, but I could tell by now they were thinning out.

I kept a more careful watch behind us and to the sides, as did Taika.

It seemed to take hours, and in the end even Veldi slumped against the wall, the portcullis now firmly down, and the floor littered with broken stone.

"They're not resetting," Taika said, looking out over the battlefield. "There's thousands of spirits still left, trapped here, though."

"But not as many as there were?" Yagmar asked. "Why?"

I knew the answer to that, but let Taika respond. "To animate a statue like that, you'd need to bind a spirit to it. These spirits were probably trapped here partly for that purpose."

"Only partly? What would be the rest of it?"

Taika just shook his head. "I have a bad feeling that we're going to find out."

Thirty-One
Breaking Bonds

"What happened to the spirits that were in the statues?" Veldi asked.

"Same as a person, I'd guess. Once the vessel has been destroyed, they go on to whatever afterlife a spirit has."

"Spirits have an afterlife?" Veldi asked.

"I thought spirits were the afterlife," Yagmar said at the same time.

I glanced at Niala, who seemed to be ignoring the conversation altogether.

"No," Taika answered. "They're a completely different thing than people. Unless they possess someone, or are forced into an object, they never incorporate. As far I know, they never age or die normally either."

"So, we just killed a bunch of immortal beings," Yagmar said, with a touch of sadness that surprised me.

"It was a mercy. At this point, I'd imagine they'd be yearning for death," Taika said.

I wondered, though. They may have been trapped here for a thousand years, but what's a thousand years to an immortal? I didn't say anything of course, though I might make an alternate ending to the song. After a rollicking fight, a melancholy ending might be the right choice for certain audiences.

Rollicking. Is that would it be? The song I would write telling the tale of this fight would make it sound exciting. Maybe fun. I didn't know how I could capture the terror that it really was. Could I convey the truth of the moment? I could make an audience laugh, or cry. I wondered if I could truly make them afraid. Make them feel the fear that I still felt. That'd be a real challenge.

After a short hike, the hall passed through another doorway with a raised portcullis. The windlass for this one was on the side we came from. It opened into another large chamber with five doorways around it, counting the one we had come through. The walls were covered at all levels with even more bas relief sculptures of soldiers in various poses and writing at all angles.

The sculptures here were different than the others. There was no cohesion between them. Each stood in its own vignette. One was standing, staring out at something, his hand shading his eyes. Another digging in the ground with a shovel. Another seemed to be felling a tree, and yet another was pulling down on a rope that rose up and out of frame.

The writing was the strangest of it all. Instead of the neat lines of inscriptions we had seen before, it wound around, snaking through the chamber, across walls, ceiling, and even the floor in strange intertwining patterns.

Veldi eyed the raised portcullises suspiciously. "Which way from here, do you think?" She asked nobody in particular.

"It's music again," I said. "Dozens of different songs—they each wind around and branch off through different doorways. I have no idea which is the right one, though."

"We're outside the wards!" Taika suddenly exclaimed.

I turned to look at him.

"They end at the doorway. We can use magic here. May I?"

Veldi thought for a moment, then asked, "What are you planning on doing?"

"Looking at these runes to see if they're connected to anything."

"Go ahead."

"*Taravakan oshir*," he said, and reached out his hand while facing one of the inscriptions.

"Well?" Veldi said, after about a minute of us all staring at Taika waiting for him to say something.

"I think...Yes. Oghni? Can you play the first bit of, how about, this one?" He pointed to one of the runic inscriptions.

I plucked the first few strings as I had before, hurrying to do what he'd asked before Veldi could veto it.

"Keep going," Taika said. "It should—"

He stopped when it became obvious what it should do. The letters began glowing. First the ones I played, then another batch next to them.

"Keep going," Taika said again, excitedly.

Nobody else said anything, so I continued. Another batch of runes lit up, and then another when I got to the end of those.

"That should be good," he said.

"Yeah, I think we can see what it's doing, but..."

"How to choose the right place to start," He finished for me. "I don't know."

I looked over the hundreds of bars of notation in despair. I had no idea which one was the right start.

"Here," Niala said, pointing at a bas-relief carving depicting a man in a traveling cloak and holding a large staff with a forked top. He had one foot forward as if he were setting out on the road.

Directly beneath the figure was a bar of musical notation. I lifted the crwth again, and played the notes listed.

They lit up, half a dozen at a time, as I played. The glowing inscriptions snaked their way down the wall, across the floor, and to one of the doorways. I stepped closer to each new group as I went.

"Wait," Taika said, as I was about to step over the threshold. "The wards are still up on that side."

I stopped playing. As I did, the glyphs in front of me faded and went out.

"Now what?" I asked.

Nobody responded.

"We can't use magic," I said, thinking it through out loud. "But I wasn't using magic. Just playing music. The magic was embedded..."

I didn't know enough to know how it worked, or what we could do safely.

Taika's brow was furrowed as he mulled it over himself.

"We know which way to go now," Niala said, and darted through the door. She sprinted down the hallway in front of us.

"Wait!" Veldi yelled after her. I agreed. We had no idea what further dangers lay ahead.

Niala ignored her, though, and disappeared around a corner.

I was about to go after her when Yagmar brushed by me and ran down the same passage.

"Dammit," I heard Veldi say behind me. "Fine, let's get after those fools."

The three of them began moving carefully in the direction that Niala and Yagmar had ran in.

I was about to go after them, but then I had an idea. The musical inscriptions had been showing the way. They continued in the corridor, snaking around in all directions, intertwining as they did in the room. There had to be a reason for it.

I went back to the first inscription and began playing again.

With what limited information I had, I knew I wasn't using any magic myself. My hands, so to speak, were nowhere near the veil. Anything opening it had to be confined to the inscriptions themselves on the way, listening for specific music and glowing in response. However it worked, I assumed the one performing the music would be safe.

Unless it was a trap, I thought to myself as I approached the doorway, in which case I was about to step into it.

I stepped into it.

My foot landed on the other side of the doorway into the hall, and nothing happened. I realized I was standing under a heavy portcullis with rather pronounced steel spikes on the bottom and took another step forward, out from under it.

I continued playing, and more inscriptions began glowing as I slowly moved forward, following them.

It was less than a minute before I ran into Veldi, Taika, and Lonto, together coming back toward me with great haste.

Thirty-Two

The Singer and the Staff

"You figured it out," Veldi said, seeing the glowing glyphs on the wall ahead of me. "Keep playing and you'll see what I mean."

I just nodded and continued.

The four of us followed the glowing path revealed by the sound as I plucked the strings of my crwth.

The path branched, and we followed the way the glowing letters went. It branched again and we did the same.

I continued to hope this whole thing wasn't deliberately leading us into a trap.

After a third branch, as the tunnel we were in straightened out and the inscriptions were lined up on the floor in three neat columns, instead of snaking around. I wasn't sure what to make of this, until one by one the lines in the right-most column started glowing. After about a dozen lines, it switched to the left-most column, and I heard Yagmar's call from up ahead.

"Oghni? Is that you? Are the others with you?"

Veldi lifted her lantern, and we saw that right after the glowing characters switched columns, the floor had given way.

"Careful, there's a bit of drop," Yagmar called.

I approached the edge and looked over. Dimly in the lantern's light, at the bottom of a deep pit, Yagmar stood, looking up.

"I'm uninjured," he called, "But I can't climb up. I hope you brought a rope."

"We found the safe passage, thanks to Oghni's music," Veldi said to him, once he had climbed the rope up. "What did you find?"

"I found this," Yagmar said, and handed her a small smooth stone with violet and gold paint. I recognized it immediately.

"It's the stone I gave Niala!" I said. "I found it in the river where we camped by the waterfall."

"So, Niala went this way?" Veldi said.

"I don't think so," Yagmar replied. "I think she wanted us to think she did, though."

"Explain!" I demanded.

He gave me a sympathetic look. "It's not finished, right?"

There was some paint on it, bright violet and gold, in an abstract pattern. It was far from complete, though. She had told me that parts could only be done under certain phases of the moon. It was a complex formula, and different for every stone.

"Right," I said.

"Something identifiably hers, but not valuable to her."

That hurt. It was a gift from me. I would hope that alone would carry some value.

"You're saying she discarded it to lure you down the wrong pathway."

"Which she somehow knew was the wrong pathway and knew the floor would collapse when I stepped on it. It's the only explanation for where it was when I found it."

"If she knows that much, she must somehow know the right path," Veldi said.

"Agreed," Yagmar said. "And I take it you do, too, now?" he looked at me. I nodded in response.

"Then what are we waiting for?" He asked.

For it to make sense, I thought, then realized it wouldn't. Not until we'd caught up to her. She had been holding something back, and now she had deliberately lured Yagmar into a trap.

We followed the path.

We came to another chamber. Two large creatures, bipedal with clawed hands and enormous sharp teeth, lay dead by the entry way. Killed very recently by very precise knife wounds. A pillar, surrounded by shattered stone, jutted from a raised circle in the center of the room.

"She got the staff," Veldi said.

I whirled on her. "What staff?" I asked, very quietly.

Out of the corner of my eye, I could see Yagmar had dropped his hand to his axe, though he hadn't drawn it.

Lonto turned slightly, stepping back and dropped into a ready pose, preparing to back Veldi. I thought for a second of reaching for my own dagger, or my crwth, but Veldi held her hands out in a placating manner.

"Yes. I knew about it," she said. "Yes, I didn't tell you. We can fight about it, or stand around casting recriminations, or we can stop her before she gets away with it."

"What is it?" Yagmar asked before I could. "What makes this one staff so important?"

"It was used by Rhogna. It's the secret to his success in battle."

"How does it work?" He asked.

"I don't know," Veldi responded. "But—"

"Warsong," I said. "Whatever it does, it attacks the will. It's how warsong works, only much, much stronger. The statues we fought were probably animated with its power. A trap laid a thousand years ago with magic so powerful it can imbue will to stone."

"That doesn't sound good," Yagmar said.

"He used it to conquer half the world," I reminded them. I could feel all eyes on me and for once I didn't like it. "Niala...I don't know what she wants it for. As far as I know she doesn't have an army. You," I rounded on Veldi, "were planning on using it for revenge against the king, I take it."

"What part of *we need to move* wasn't clear?" Veldi said, and pushed past us, back the way we'd come. Nobody got in her way. "I'll explain everything later, I swear," she called behind her, then broke into a sprint down the corridor. The rest of us followed her. She had lied to us, but Niala had betrayed us. Betrayed me. I had to know why.

I ran after her.

We found more statues, broken along the way, and another of the strange beasts. The blood was still flowing out of its neck as it lay on the ground. If it wasn't dead, it would be soon. Its teeth were longer than my forearm, and I was glad I missed the fight.

"Hopefully, it at least slowed her down," Veldi said.

Lonto hadn't spoken, but I was used to that.

Taika hadn't declared a side in our standoff back in the staff grotto.

The Grotto of the Staff I called it in my head, thinking of how to tell the story and only hating myself a little bit for doing so at a time like this.

When we got back to the beginning of the music chamber, the portcullis in the doorway leading into it was down.

Thirty-Three
Death and Betrayal

"I'll get it," Lonto said and, without waiting for a response, transformed. He reached forward and became a large snake that slithered through the bars.

We could do nothing but stand and watch as the snake made its way, quicker than I would have thought, through the rubble that littered the path, to the windlass that raised the portcullis.

Just as he reached it, though, Niala, my love, my betrayer, stepped out from around the corner, knife in each hand. With a single smooth motion, severed the snake's head.

I stood, frozen in disbelief. I heard someone shout behind me, then Yagmar was next to me, trying to lift the heavy gate by hand.

Veldi joined him, then Taika.

Niala looked to me, and our eyes met. She said nothing, but wore a look of profound sadness. Which only increased both my anger and my confusion.

The body of the snake thrashed about. Niala reached into her tunic and pulled out the bag of spirit stones. She retrieved one and placed it next to the lifeless snake that had been Lonto.

With a single fluid motion, Yagmar drew one of his throwing axes and sent it through the air toward her. She ducked out of its way, but it struck the bag, spilling the stones across the floor. A flash of anger crossed her face, then, but she turned to run, disappearing around the corner.

"Go!" I heard Yagmar yell.

Before I knew what was happening, Taika pushed me forward, ducking under the raised portcullis.

I followed him, then turned to hold it up as best I could as first Veldi moved under it then, the three of us holding it up, barely kept it from crushing Yagmar as he let go and dove under it himself.

He sprinted forward and the rest of us followed. When we reached Lonto's corpse, there was no sign of Niala. Yagmar stopped briefly and swept the stones into the bag.

Veldi stood, sword at the ready, watching over us. It only took a few seconds, and then Yagmar handed me the bag.

"Me?" I said in astonishment.

"Probably better than anyone else to figure out what to do with the damn things. If nothing else, you can always sell them."

Sell them. Like it was a casual thing. I probably could, to the right buyer. They'd be worth a fortune. One of these was probably more wealth than in my entire village. Of course, selling even one would attract the attention of the priesthood of Arakthala, so I'd have to be careful.

Who was I kidding. I was never going to do that.

I didn't recognize the pattern on the stone she'd left with the snake corpse of Lonto. I glanced back again while Yagmar pulled me away. I realized I had been expecting him to turn back into his human form when he died. For all I knew, though, that was just another shape he assumed. Maybe the snake was his true form. Perhaps he had no true form. Whatever he was, I felt something was lost from the world with his passing, beyond the man I had traveled with for the better part of a fortnight but never truly came to know.

Veldi grabbed the stone that had been left with him and tossed it back to me. "Whatever her plans for him were, he lived on his own terms, and he deserves to make his own decisions about where he goes next."

I shuddered as I placed the soul stone back into the bag. What would happen to me, I wondered, if I died with the entire bag in my possession? Would the minions of Arakthala ignore them? Or choose from among the ones present? Or was there more to it than merely placing the stone? By the river, she had seemed to indicate that that was all it took.

Perhaps they had to be removed from the bag to work.

I hastily dropped the stone back into the bag, before tucking it into a pocket. I ran to catch up to my remaining friends.

Yagmar was waiting at the bottom of a rope when I caught up to them. He motioned for me to climb, and I didn't hesitate to do so. He began right after me. So much for the one at a time rule, I guess.

Outside, my heart broke all over again. The Tyroth was gone. Our provisions were scattered and burnt. She'd wasted no time. A huge fire, a thick column of smoke rising to the sky, was in full blaze.

"They'll know where we are," Veldi said.

"I can put it out," Taika said.

"Do it."

I shifted to the veilsight to see what he was doing. With all the snow piled around, I almost expected him to dump a mass of it onto the fire. That would have left steam and smoke rising, though.

Instead, he opened a small portal—I couldn't see to where—and just pulled the whole fire through it. In a second, it had vanished, leaving nothing behind but the half-burnt fuel, not even smoldering. On a hunch, I leaned forward. It was cold to the touch, as if it had been out for days.

I looked up at Taika, who was beaming with pride.

"You'll have to show me that one some time," I told him.

"Nice. Let's get out of here before anyone finds us," Veldi said.

"She'll head east, over the mountain," Yagmar said as we left.

"And without our supplies, we'll have to go back to Ravens Feast before we can follow her," Veldi said. "Which is why she destroyed everything she didn't take."

"Can we? Even then? With the king's soldiers looking for us, and winter closing in..."

"I don't see much choice," Veldi said. "If we don't stop her..."

We'd eventually end up facing an army of Shar'i'nol coming over the mountains. I was tempted to let that be the king's problem and head back home to my farm.

But I've never once sung a song that ended with someone giving up and going home. Besides, war would find us there, too.

I thought of my grandmother's sword, hanging over the mantle. Would mine someday hang over my own grandchildren's?

We shouldered our packs and the gear we had taken into the caves with us and began moving through the snow on foot. Without the Tyroth, it would take us half a fortnight at least before we reached Ravens Feast.

Thirty-Four
A New Direction

The first day, we marched mostly in silence. My crwth spent the day slung on my back. My mind was far too troubled for music. Nobody broached the subject of what we were going to do now. Somewhere behind us, in an undiscovered part of the tomb, lay the lost treasure of Rhogna the conqueror. The treasure that, ostensibly, we had traveled all this way to retrieve. Nobody spoke of it. Nobody spoke of Niala, either, though I thought of nothing else. She betrayed me. She betrayed all of us. I concentrated on the falling snow.

East or west would be the decision we'd have to make. Niala almost certainly went east. We wouldn't have to decide until we got to Ravens Feast.

Yagmar and Veldi went to hunt something for dinner. We'd have to make camp every night, and we'd need a fire, shelter, and to forage for food and firewood. Niala had a head start on us and could move much faster. We'd been careful with our rations on the way in, taking our time to forage for what we needed, and now she had everything, and we had to do the same out of necessity on the way back out.

That night, sitting around a somehow cheerless fire, Yagmar finally broached the subject. "You ready to talk?" he asked Veldi.

"You mean the staff," she replied. The one subject that must have been on everybody's mind throughout the day, however we tried to avoid it.

"You knew it was there." Yagmar said. I'd never heard him seem so emotionless before.

"Yes," she replied.

Nobody said anything else, so I spoke up. "Was Niala right, then? You planned to use it against the king?"

Veldi looked down before raising her head again. "Yes," she said again. "Vengeance was my goal and is the reason why I stole the ring. The book was unclear, but I knew the key depended on music, which is why I brought Oghni in. I don't know how Niala found out about it, but I guess I know why she wanted to join us. She must have been following me for a while, too."

"The staff was from her people. Rhogna was Shar'i'nol," I told them.

"What?" Veldi exclaimed.

"How do you know?" Yagmar asked.

Taika remained silent, looking between us all.

"Why didn't you tell me this before?" Veldi asked. I just gave her a look that expressed exactly what I thought of her, of all people, castigating anyone for keeping secrets.

"I didn't know until we got into the tomb," I replied. "There's a song among the Shar'i'nol about being driven out of the East into the desert long ago. They believe there is nothing to the East anymore but ruins. Rhogna couldn't have come from there." I didn't think this was the time to mention the song called it an abode of dragons.

"How sure are you of this?" Veldi asked me.

"I'm guessing on a lot of it, but I have good reason to think I'm right." I continued. "Rhogna never conquered the desert, not because they outwitted his armies, but because they were his to begin with. His plan, I think, was to conquer the West and use it

— either its armies or its economic power — to return and retake their ancient homeland. But he was defeated before he could go back. His loyal followers took his staff and built the tomb to house it. I don't believe you could use the staff," I said to Veldi. "You have to have knowledge both of magic and music, and I don't think you know enough of either to activate it. It was a fool's errand from the beginning."

"Niala's not a wizard," Yagmar said.

"Neither am I," I said.

"Neither was Lonto," Taika said. He was staring into the fire and hadn't spoken until now, but he'd obviously been listening.

I continued. "She's some other tradition, then, but they may teach magic differently in the desert. I think she's used it to extend her life. The Shar'i'nol aren't as long lived as your people, Yagmar. Otherwise, they wouldn't think of something a thousand years ago as ancient history. It would be living memory for the eldest among them."

"She uses magic when she fights, too," Taika said. He looked up toward me. "I saw an aura I didn't recognize. I thought at first that it was an effect of your battlesong, but I think now that it was something she was generating herself. It makes her faster and helps turn aside blows."

"Convenient that," Yagmar said. There was nothing but admiration in his voice. They'd known each other for two hundred years. I wondered if this was even the first time one of them had betrayed the other.

"What about the rest of the treasure?" Taika said, after a moment. "If the staff's useless, who cares if she has it instead of us? But the legends say there are piles of gold and gems within the tomb. Surely, it's worth going back for that, right? With that much money, you could find another way to get to King Ta'an."

"The staff's not useless, though," Yagmar began.

"Right," Veldi said. "Oghni could use it."

"Me? It's powerful magic. You want I should become Oghni the Conqueror? Spread suffering, famine, and pestilence throughout the nine kingdoms until they finally have enough and band together to kill me? No thanks."

"You could still..."

"It would take a while to raise that much," Taika continued his earlier thoughts. "The traps in the tomb must have taken years for them to put together and would have had to be renewed over the centuries."

"I'm less worried about Oghni the Conqueror than I am about Niala the Conqueror," Yagmar said, ignoring him. "If we don't stop her, she could use it to raise an army of her own, and we'll either be forced to deal with her then or flee before them."

"It's agreed, then? We're going after the staff?" Veldi asked.

"Even though you can't use it?" I asked. I had a sneaky suspicion she hadn't given up, and that part of her plan still involved me. "Just to be clear, if we're stopping her from raising an unholy army and decimating the kingdom with it, it won't be to allow you to raise an unholy army and decimate the kingdom with it. You won't be able to force me to use the staff on your behalf. If I could use it, which is by no means certain, the first thing I would do is turn its power against you. And anybody else you could find — and I'm sure there are others — would have even less loyalty to you than I do, and do the same as soon as they realized they don't need you."

I was looking directly into her eyes as I said it, and I could see her blanch.

From the corner of my eye, I could see Yagmar nod in approval, which was a bigger relief than I was ready to admit.

Taika still stayed quiet, looking back and forth between us. He didn't want to take sides in this, and I couldn't blame him. If it came to a fight, I wondered if he'd stay out of it, or take Veldi's side. I couldn't see him taking mine.

I had no doubt that Yagmar could beat Veldi, but I'd likely be dead before it was finished.

Thirty-Five
Blood in the Snow

Finally, Veldi nodded. "I understand," she said. "But you're right that it's the kingdoms who'll suffer if another army under the sway of Rhogna's staff were to make its way across the mountains. I'll postpone my vengeance long enough to help you track it down, and see if we can destroy it. If we don't, then there'll be a hundred more like Naheela. Agreed? Once that's done, we can discuss our next steps and whether you want to take them with me."

I nodded. "Sounds good to me," I said.

"None of you are a match for her," Yagmar said. "And I want an explanation."

"As do I," I agreed.

"Lonto was my friend," Taika said.

"East it is, then, once we reach Ravens Feast," I confirmed.

Nobody else said anything. We still had several days to go.

We never made it.

For the next few days, things had gone back mostly to how they were in our earlier journey, although completely different. Nobody joked. No songs were sung. We spent the day walking, the nights camping. Taika and Yagmar build new snow shelters each night, then Taika and I foraged for wood for the fire while Veldi and Yagmar hunted for our dinner. Breakfast and lunch were whatever was left over from dinner the previous night. It was slow going and we were aware that Niala would be furthering her lead every day.

Still, we pressed on.

It was the fourth night, and we estimated we were only a couple of days away, when I was awakened by a scream.

I opened my eyes and blinked in the darkness. A large figure dove past me, and I realized it was Yagmar. With his axe in both hands, he rolled out the small doorway of our shelter, tearing the fabric we'd hung up over it. Through a flurry of snow, I could see firelight coming from outside.

I grabbed my crwth and followed him out, a bit slower, and Taika was right behind me. Veldi was on watch, but I saw no sign of her as I exited.

An arrow flew from the darkness ahead of us and buried itself up to the fletching in the snow of our shelter. It had passed less than a hand span from me.

"Taika!" Yagmar bellowed as he charged forward. I moved to the side, trying to get out of the firelight, barely registering the cold against my bare feet. I'd grabbed my crwth, not my cloak and boots. But we were under attack, and I could deal with cold feet for a couple of minutes. I hoped.

Taika cast his spell, and half a dozen figures hidden amongst the trees glowed palely.

Yagmar charged toward the first, who was desperately trying to load a crossbow.

Two others were close to finishing doing the same and I strummed a tune that made them skip a beat on the windlass, just enough to slow them down for a second.

It was enough. Yagmar brought his axe upward as he went, cleaving the man's belly and weapon in one motion, before taking three more steps to bring it back down, deep into another man's head, right through his helmet. He used his foot to pry it back out just as another one sprung at him, sword in hand.

Another of our attackers had finished reloading her crossbow and was taking aim.

I ran my bow across the strings, shifting the music just enough to confuse her, moving her aim from Yagmar to the swordsman in front of him.

She jerked the crossbow at the last second, missing her companion barely. It was enough of a distraction, though, that Yagmar could get past his guard and crush his throat with the tip of his axe.

The soldier with the crossbow started reloading again while frantically looking around. Sighting Taika, she shifted her attention to him and raised her weapon before dropping it again, both hands flying to her throat. She desperately clawed at it before she toppled backwards into the snow.

Taika looked winded from the strain.

I glanced back over to see how Yagmar was doing, and he'd dispatched another opponent, who was now lying in the snow beside two fragments of his shattered sword.

Yagmar was headed toward one of the two remaining figures. The other hadn't emerged from hiding yet, though we could all see the faint outline from Taika's spell.

The one standing man braced his spear, ready to meet Yagmar's charge. I changed music again, and convinced the tree he was standing under to bend its branch ever so slightly, just enough to dump its entire load of snow directly onto his head. It didn't hurt him, but surprised him and obscured his vision long enough for

Yagmar to step to one side of the spear, and spin almost all the way around before burying his axe into his back.

At that moment, I heard three things, simultaneously. The faint twang of a crossbow being released behind us, a scream of pain from Taika, and the blast of a horn from a hiding, now fleeing, figure.

"I got 'em, help the kid!" Yagmar yelled at me as he charged forward into the forest. If this were a song, I'd describe him as consumed by barbarian rage.

I got to Taika and found him down in the snow, a crossbow bolt embedded in his lower leg. Which meant somewhere where I couldn't see was someone with a crossbow. I didn't know Taika's spell for illuminating our enemies.

"Can you mark him for me?" I asked. "Just hold on a little bit. Yagmar will be back in a second, and once this guy's dealt with, I can see to your wound."

He just nodded, then cast his spell, accompanied by another cry of pain.

I saw him. He was in a good defensible position. I didn't have a crossbow, and even if I did his would release before mine. He was taking aim again and there was no close shelter we could dive behind. I had to act fast.

I drew the bow across my lute strings, a loud discordant note then sawed back and forth, playing as quickly as I could. I spoke the words at the same time and twisted my mind down the strange paths needed to open the veil. It was a variant of the same spell I used to dry mine and Niala's clothes by the pond before our first kiss. Before she betrayed me and fled. I used my anger and my grief to power the spell, putting everything I had into it. I'd assisted in many fights, but I'd never directly killed anyone with magic before. I didn't hold back now. There was no other way to get to him in time.

He shrieked as he died, a pitiful wailing as all the water in his head dissipated out, leaving a dried husk above his shoulders. He didn't even fall; he was supported too well in his hiding spot. But there could be no doubt he was dead.

Yagmar reached us a moment later.

"You alright?" he asked me. I just nodded, out of breath. He turned to Taika. "Can you help him?" He asked me.

"Yes," I turned my attention to Taika. The bolt was in deep, I looked through veilsight, and could see it had chipped the bone. I could heal the wound if I pulled it out, but it would take a while. Unfortunately, I also saw something else: Mage eaters circling around him. My spell had been a beacon to them. We'd have to get him out of here before we could do anything.

"Oh no. No no no!" I heard Yagmar cry. I looked over in time to see him drop to his knees in the snow near something I couldn't make out. I had a horrid suspicion about what it was, though.

Thirty-Six
A Ration of Magic

I looked over to him, then back to Taika.

"You can't do anything for me here," he said. He would have already been aware of the mage eaters. "Go to Yagmar."

With a last apologetic look, I did. When I got there, I saw what I'd feared. Veldi, lying in the snow. A bolt from a crossbow, probably the first one fired, had pierced her chest. She'd have had enough time to scream before she died, and that was likely it. A second or two after she'd known, she was dead. There was nothing anyone could do for her now.

Maybe.

I drew out the bag of soul stones. Aside from the black stone, I wasn't sure what any of them did.

"Do you know which—" I started, but he cut me off.

"None," he said. "She's earned her afterlife. Let her go on her own terms. She wouldn't thank you for saving her with anything from her betrayer."

He didn't even want to say Niala's name. They'd been friends for two hundred years. I couldn't even imagine what her betrayal must meant to him. They had been lovers, long before she met me. Veldi was his current one, and Niala had caused her death.

I didn't know what to say to any of that.

"Can Taika walk yet?" he asked me.

I shook my head. "Mage eaters. We have to get away from here before we can fix his leg."

"Dammit," he swore. "More delays, right when we can least afford them."

I snapped a look at him.

He understood what I wanted to know. "These guys had the king's livery under their cloaks. That horn was probably to let the rest of the soldiers know they'd found us."

"How many of them?"

"No idea. More than we can defeat. Especially without magic."

"I can—" Taika started.

"You can wait until we're out of danger, is what you can do. Sorry we don't have time to make a litter. Try not to scream too loudly." At this, he scooped up the young wizard and began walking. "Half a league, you say?"

"At least," I replied. "Farther would be better."

Taika winced in pain, but kept quiet, his lips tightly flattened.

We didn't make it half a league.

We barely made it half that before we saw our pursuers. A dozen soldiers, maybe more, all mounted on thick beasts who trod upon the snow on four short legs with wide soft feet.

"There!" Taika gasped. "Get to that rock outcropping!"

Yagmar burst into a sprint, and I followed closely behind him.

The soldiers were upon us before we made it, even in our mad scramble through the thick snow.

Yagmar threw Taika in a great heave into a snowbank.

Taika landed with a stifled whimper of pain.

Yagmar hefted his axe, turning to face our enemies.

I drew my dagger, not daring to risk magic with the mage eaters so close.

"No, go get the kid to that rock shelf. I think I know what he's planning, and I can handle these guys," Yagmar growled.

As if in answer, another horn sounded in the distance.

Yagmar barked a wry laugh at that. "Or I can hold them off for a bit. Hopefully, long enough."

I nodded and sheathed my dagger, then made my way as quickly as I could to Taika, who was doing his best to crawl through the waist-deep snow.

I helped him to his feet and half carried, half dragged him to the spot he indicated.

"There," he said, pointing up hill from us and off to the side. "Help me up."

I saw what he was planning. "Can you? There are mage eaters still..."

"It's gonna hurt. With luck, I'll pass out and only wake up when we're leagues away and you can safely use your magic to heal me again."

I just nodded and helped him to his feet.

Below us, Yagmar had killed four of the soldiers, but was being pressed back by the other four.

Another dozen, at least, were approaching, and who knew how many behind them. The king knew about the staff and wouldn't be content on just killing Veldi. I didn't know what would happen if they caught us, and I didn't want to find out.

"Yagmar!" I shouted. "Now!"

He stepped back then, retreating from the battle, still fighting, blocking blows from the three remaining soldiers.

The fools would have been wiser to let him go.

I drew my dagger then and threw it at one of the men. It struck him but didn't penetrate his armor.

It was enough, though, to be a distraction. He flinched away from it, giving Yagmar an opening. The large axe swung upward and caught him below the chin before pushing inward and back down, opening his throat and half his chest.

Another soldier thrust forward but Yagmar dove into a roll, forward, under his sweep, taking the soldier's leg out from under him as he went. He was now further down the slope. Beside me, Taika was mumbling to himself, repeating the words of a spell. There was a ward interwoven with it. Tricky to do both at once, but it gave Yagmar more time if he was able to get up.

I could also sense the mage eaters gathering around us.

I told myself the kid knew what he was doing.

I hoped the kid knew what he was doing.

I wanted to invoke the veilsight, but I didn't dare. I was using both hands holding Taika upright, and without my crwth, anything I did magically would just attract more spirits. I could already feel them beginning to pull at me. I realized too late what was happening. Taika wasn't warding himself with his spell, he was warding me.

"No!" I cried out, "You can't—"

"It's the only way," he said. "I already can barely walk. If we're both down, we all die."

I hated it, but he was right. I kept him up. It was the least I could do. He continued his spell. Even without the veilsight, I could tell what he was doing: It was a variation of the water spell. Only, instead of gathering water, he was consolidating the snow, pulling it together, melting it. Not all of it, just a small patch. The snow at the bottom of the great drift covering a mountainside.

With its foundation suddenly turned to water, it fell. And when it fell, it pulled the rest down with it. The noise of the rumbling tumbling snow was deafening. I'd never seen or heard an avalanche before. The snow fell, in front of us, and two dozen soldiers and their mounts all perished, buried beneath it. Their screams barely audible over the noise of the mountain of snow falling on them all at once.

It was a horrible death. Crushed or suffocating, I wouldn't wish it on anyone.

I reconsidered that. They were planning on killing us after all.

Yagmar barely avoided it himself, running up the slope to us in our sheltered position.

"That was close!" he exclaimed.

Taika looked up at him, opened his mouth as if to say something, and promptly collapsed to the ground.

Thirty-Seven
Up and Out

It was six hours later when Taika awoke.

Yagmar had been carrying him the whole time, as we trudged through the snow, pursued by horns in the distance.

"How many soldiers did they send after us?" I grumbled.

"How many would you send to retrieve an artifact that would cost you your kingdom if lost?" Yagmar responded.

All the rest of the day we continued, making our way as fast as we could. Taika offered to erase our tracks, but Yagmar pointed out it wouldn't be worth it. "They've almost certainly brought another wizard by now, and we left a lot of our own possessions back there."

I didn't point out that we also left a lot of blood, which a skilled wizard could do some really horrible stuff with if they got hold of it, which they almost certainly would.

"I guess there's only one way we could have gone anyway," Taika said.

It was true. Maybe we could have scaled the hillside here, but if we were to have any chance to survive, we had to take the quickest route. Leaving the road, such as it was, would slow us so much our pursuers would certainly catch us.

So, we stuck to the path, pushing against the snow, with the horns blowing in the distance. In the narrow canyon we were traveling through now it was impossible to tell how far away they were, or if they were getting closer or not.

"You're going to have to make a decision about which way to go once we reach Ravens Feast," Yagmar said.

"I thought we'd already decided on east," I said. "Why is it my decision now?"

"You were more wronged by her than any of us," Taika said.

I thought of Veldi, lying dead in the snow, and Lonto, left in the tomb in his snake form. I looked back to Yagmar, who had loved both Veldi and Niala, and had been friends with Niala since before anyone I'd ever met had been born, and to Taika, nearly dead from the risks he took to save us. "I'm not sure—"

Yagmar interrupted me. "Either way, you hired us so, like it or not, that makes you the leader."

"Fine, I'm still soliciting opinions. What do you think we should do?"

"I don't have anywhere else to go," Taika said. "I'll go wherever you decide."

"I hadn't thought of that. No reason for us to all go the same place," I said. "We were gathered to hunt the treasure. Without that, what keeps us together? Maybe it would be safer if we split up."

"You could turn your back on everything. Head to Pendwy. Sell those rocks you're carrying and use the money to buy your little house near the big inn."

Soul stones were near legendary. Selling a single one could set me up for life, and I had six of them. I could retire. We all could. Right here in my pocket was the means to achieve everything I'd been dreaming of.

But it was too early. I hadn't seen enough of the world yet. And there was another reason.

"I have to know," I said out loud. "I'm going east. You don't have to come with me."

"I'll come," Taika said. "If you'll have me."

"Of course," I said. "But it'll probably be more danger and less treasure along the way."

"Less than zero?" he said with a wry grin. "Don't care. I haven't been over the mountains before and besides," he gave a little shrug, "It's not like I have somewhere else to be."

"Thank you," I said, and meant it.

"You two will get lost stumbling around the mountains," Yagmar said. "And neither of you will last ten seconds in a fight."

I was about to say something. I don't know what, but I'm sure it would have been profound. Instead, I was interrupted by a horn blast, closer than any had been before.

Worse yet, it was coming from in front of us, instead of behind.

Yagmar swore by some god I'd never heard of. "They're too close. Up! Up the embankment. Maybe we can hide up there."

There was a rocky outcropping. I didn't like it but couldn't see any better option. It didn't look big enough to hide, but it was better than sitting down here waiting for two groups of soldiers to slaughter us.

We scrambled again up the snowy hill. Halfway up to the ledge Yagmar had pointed out, we were high enough up that I could see the approaching army. There weren't the two dozen soldiers we feared, there were scores. Maybe as many as a hundred.

"This is insane," I shouted over the wind. "Maybe we can reason with them?"

"Better chance of flying away than that," he said.

Taika began to say something but was interrupted by another horn blast. Different this time.

They'd spotted us.

Also, something else.

"The wind's picking up!" I shouted. "Maybe it'll get bad enough we can still lose them."

"Just as likely to lose ourselves," Yagmar growled. I looked back over to Taika and saw him mumbling under his breath. Was he bringing the wind? That would be powerful magic with wide-ranging effects. It was dangerous, but it would make things difficult for our pursuers as well. We kept going, in a mad scramble through blowing snow.

By the time we got to a ledge where I could stabilize myself enough to look back, I could barely see five paces in front of me. The armies were lost to sight.

I looked over to Taika and saw him shaking like crazy.

"Hey!" I shouted. "It's enough! You can stop!"

Yagmar looked back to see what I was talking about, and immediately leapt to his side. He caught Taika as he fell to the ground with a whimper.

Yagmar had him in hand, so I unslung my crwth and ran my bow across it, first trying to look at the situation to see what I could see. I nearly dropped it. Mage eaters, dozens of them, pulling at the kid. He had shut down the magical conduit, but it was nearly too late. I could tell parts of his insides were gone. The bones in both his legs were nearly liquid. He needed help, and I wasn't sure that I could give it to him, even if we did manage to get away from here. If it was just me doing the work, it would likely be a fortnight or more of painful knitting him back together before he was whole enough to do the rest on his own.

"No more magic," I said. "He won't survive it. He can't even walk now. You'll need to carry him."

Yagmar nodded and scooped him up, as he had done before. "Which way?" he asked me.

I looked out over the pass. The wind was already dying down, and there were people, large numbers of them, approaching from both sides. They'd converge within minutes.

"Up," I said, gesturing. "The road is closed to us."

"Alright," he replied, and begin pushing forward through the deep snow. "Can you make it?"

"Gonna have to," I told him.

Thirty-Eight
From Snow to Sand, and Dust

Going downhill just made us targets. Going up was our only chance. A slim one at best, but all we had.

The snow was still falling, but the wind had died down. I struggled forward, half climbing up the hill, going from boulder to boulder, ledge to ledge.

I could tell Taika was doing his best to stay quiet, but he still whimpered and moaned as Yagmar struggled up the hill ahead of me, carrying him.

I was amazed at his strength. Even burdened as he was, I was falling behind. I tried to stay quiet, too, to avoid distracting him. I didn't want to die here, but I didn't want to be left alone, either.

An arrow struck the rock I was pulling myself up onto. I turned and could see the archer. He was a long way away and firing near the end of his range. It was just luck that his arrow even came as close as it did, but the next one might be even closer. We needed to do something, but all I could do was keep climbing.

We were halfway up the hill when Taika spoke again.

"Stop," he said, in a weak voice.

I looked up and saw that Yagmar stopped. He sat Taika atop a boulder, propping him up while shielding him from the soldier's arrows.

I pushed on, trying to catch up to them. More arrows fell around us. We were within range now. There was no way we could reach the top before they reached us.

"I can get you out of this," Taika said.

"No," I replied. "There are too many mage eaters around. Any more magic and you'll die."

"I might not," he told me. "This many of the king's soldiers will almost certainly have a healer with them. They'll want to interrogate me."

"Bad idea, kid," Yagmar said. "Anything less than bringing the mountain down on them isn't going to stop them. You'll just kill us all."

"Not all," Taika replied. "Worst case, I die, you two walk free. I can send you ahead."

"Open a portal?" I exclaimed. "There's no way you can do that in your current condition."

"I can," he said. "I'll probably pass out from the pain, but they'll find me."

"It's too big a risk. Even if they do take you alive, they'll kill you once they get what they want."

"It's no risk!" He insisted. "I know it's not a good option, but there are no good options. We have exactly two possibilities. Either they catch us and kill us all, or they catch just me and maybe kill me. I'll take me-maybe-dead and you both alive over me-definitely-dead and you both also. If either of you could do it, I'd let you, but you can't, so stand back and let me do what I have to."

As self-serving as it may sound, I couldn't fault his logic. The fact was, he did have a better chance on his own. I nodded and stepped back.

"If they take you, we'll do our best to mount a rescue."

Yagmar nodded his agreement. "You are the bravest man I've ever traveled with, kid. Keep a pint cold in Ta'va'stok for me."

Taika gave a feeble sort of laugh. "That's Oghni's trick," he said. "He never did show it to me. Last question: east or west?"

Yagmar looked to me. "Your call," he said. "East into certain danger, or West into wealth and luxury?"

I was tempted, but I couldn't. Not yet.

I shook my head. "I have to know why."

"That's what I thought. East it is, kid. And good luck."

Taika stood up straighter and began weaving his spell. I had never seen a portal opened before. Ilby had described how it worked, once, though he told me it was too dangerous to do without need.

I could feel the veil ripping and strummed my crwth enough to bring up the veilsight.

By the time I saw what he was doing, though, it was too late.

He opened the portal. As predicted, every spirit from leagues around came rushing toward us. He wouldn't survive this. I'd never seen such a large rend in the veil. I'd never even heard of one, outside of legend.

The portal opened, like a shimmering circle in the air around us. It enveloped Yagmar and me and began to close. As it did, I could see Taika dragged, pulled wholly into that other world where the mage eaters lived.

But the tear widened still, as Yagmar and I were pulled the opposite direction, bodily through another world, sucked inexorably through a vortex that connected back to our own. The vanguard of the advancing army was close enough that I could see the look of terror in their faces when the spirits swarmed through the tear to take all of them as well.

I saw what he did. It was one of the most powerful workings of magic I had ever heard of.

A thousand years ago, a company of wizards opposing the Conqueror stood beside a small river and ripped a continent in half. Whatever afterlife Taika was heading for, nobody would question his right to stand with them.

If he were going to sacrifice himself, it wouldn't be small. He intended to take that entire army with him. All of our pursuers: The vanguard who'd caught up to us, the others who were drawing near, and the entirety of their main host, a league away or more. All of them devoured by the spirits from the world that Taika had opened.

It would be a generation before anyone could safely work magic in the pass again.

The portal slammed shut behind me.

I fell to my knees in hot sand and cried.

I wept for all of us.

For Taika, and his bravery, and his sacrifice, and for the loss. The loss of everything he would have become and all the stories that would never come into being.

I wept for Lonto, so strange and quiet and big and gruff and gentle. For a deep rich story that I only saw the tiniest part of before it was snatched away forever.

For Veldi, who lied to us and was killed for it.

For myself, for love lost, and love betrayed. For my song of romance that would never be completed.

I wept because the gods never would.

Thirty-Nine
Waiting for an Ambush

At long last, I looked up.

A mountain range filled the horizon before me. The sun beat down and I realized the air was hot, and dry.

I turned away from the mountains and saw Yagmar standing nearby. Waiting for me to finish, no doubt. He nodded his acknowledgment. No more than that was needed. He understood.

Of course he understood. She was his friend, too. They both were. His former lover betrayed us, and his current lover lay dead by her hand. What was my grief compared to that?

"Are those the Eastern mountains?" I asked him, knowing the answer.

"They're the Western Mountains now, I suppose," he replied with a wry grin.

"Taika…" I started. I realized he wouldn't have known. He couldn't see what I had seen.

"He didn't make it, did he?"

"No."

"I suspected as much. Something in the way he said it. He knew he was going to die. He sacrificed himself for us. I hope he took some of them with him."

"I think he took all of them with him." I told him what happened, the sheer scope of it.

He looked up toward the mountains, then, as if he could see the devastation Taika had wrought from down here. "Good for you, kid."

Neither of us spoke for a long minute.

Finally, Yagmar turned to me. "If I'm right, this is the old trade road. The same one we would have been on if we'd made it to Ravens Feast. She should be coming down it in about half a fortnight. I think there's a village not too far east of here, right on the edge of the desert."

And that was that.

"Are you thinking we re-supply there, then wait?"

"Maybe hire a few people, set up an ambush."

An ambush. For Niala.

"We'll have to get the staff away from her."

We discussed strategy as we walked. Any attack and the first thing she'd do would be to go for the staff. Unless... unless she didn't really feel threatened by the attack somehow.

So that was our plan.

The village was where Yagmar remembered it.

They didn't remember him. It had been a hundred years since he'd last been this way. Before the Goblin War.

Unlike Ravens Feast, there was virtually no indication that the town had once been much larger. They had a ready supply of lumber from the nearby hills, and less means of hauling stone, so most of the buildings were made of wood. As the town shrank, they were abandoned and torn down as they began to rot away. I wondered how long it would be before it was gone entirely.

There was a small inn, and the people there were happy to see us, two travelers from the other side of the mountains.

We were not the only travelers who crossed the mountains. They'd had visitors every few fortnights for the last several years. Almost never in the winter, though.

"Why would two travelers cross the mountains alone in winter?" the innkeeper asked us.

"Sadly, we weren't alone when we started," I told him. "We had nothing but bad luck the whole time. Bandits on the west side, then strange flying creatures near the summit. Add in the usual snow and wind and a slide or two... well, most of those that weren't smart enough to turn back didn't make it."

Yagmar paid for our first night there, producing several silver coins from somewhere, keeping his pouch of gold still hidden.

The second day, I offered to perform, which the inn staff and clientele happily took me up on. They were eager to hear news and songs from across the mountains. By the end of the night, I'd managed to put aside thoughts of the gruesome business ahead of us, and my hat was full of coins. More than enough to pay for the rest of our stay myself, though Yagmar insisted on continuing to do so.

"It's my fault we're here," he said. "If I hadn't arranged her audition back in Tenn..."

"I'm the one that hired her," I said. "Our employer lied to us, too. If either of them had told us the truth..."

"Bah, recriminations are going to get us nowhere. Most likely, Veldi would've betrayed us all if Niala hadn't beaten her to it."

"No point pondering the what-ifs," I said, quoting my father, "when the what-is is bad enough."

He just nodded in response to that.

"I tell you, though," I said as I poured my earnings of the evening into a bag, "If I had known we'd get a reception like this here, I would have crossed the mountains on purpose."

Things continued like that for a few more days. Yagmar had found some kids in the village who were eager to earn a few coppers by scouting out the pass we'd come through, and report back if they saw anyone coming.

"Keep it quiet, though," he told them. "We don't want to alarm everyone." He had to offer several assurances that the village itself was in no danger.

The fact was, though, if it was in danger, we'd likely be the only ones who could stop it.

On the fifth day, he found several adults from the village willing to fight in exchange for a handful of silver.

"It'll be six of you against one of her," he told them.

He warned them she would have a magic staff, and offered a gold coin to anyone who could get it away from her. If she could be separated from the staff and taken alive it would be a gold sovereign each. It was a risk offering so much, as it let it be known that he was carrying enough wealth to make it worth killing us in our sleep.

On the eighth day his scouts came to report that a lone woman, driving a wagon pulled by a blue six-legged beast, had crossed the pass.

I was happy to hear our tyroth survived.

Forty

Blood on the Sand

Yagmar gathered his mercenaries.

I almost felt sorry for them. I had no doubt that if it was just them against Niala, they would lose, and quickly. Yagmar and I would tilt the odds against her.

I wanted to try talking to her first, but Yagmar pointed out what a bad idea that would be. Our only advantage was surprise. If she surrendered, we could talk, but she'd never surrender while she held the staff.

Yagmar hid behind one boulder. I took my position high on another, where I could signal the others of her approach.

So, I waited. And waited. No snow fell on this side of the mountains. It was hot and dry and I waited.

Eventually, there she was, sitting in the front of the cart, holding the reins of our tyroth. Just as the kids had said. I don't know why I expected her to be any different. Maybe a little more tired, a little sad, but that could just be my imagination. Maybe she was just bored from sitting behind the gentle plodding beast all day every day for eight days.

I could feel the bile rising in my gut at the sight of her. I wanted to jump out, demand an explanation, punch her in the face, or maybe just take her in my arms and kiss her while she told me there was a perfectly good explanation for everything and she never really betrayed me.

Instead, I stuck to the plan, slid out of sight, and signaled Yagmar and his little band of ruffians.

As she passed, I could see the staff, lying on the cart beside her, within easy reach. Within reach, but not going anywhere. I waited for my distraction to begin before I did my part.

After she had passed, our half-dozen hired thugs stepped out from behind the rock they were hiding behind and stood in her way. She didn't even wait for them to speak, as soon as the first one raised his crossbow, a knife flew forward and into his wrist. He dropped the crossbow with a scream of pain, and that was one out of the fight.

The other crossbow user fired. She was in motion by then, leaping forward and running up the length of the tyroth. The bolt struck the beast, and it reared up, both front legs rising higher above the ground than I'd ever seen before. Niala leapt off, turned and spun in the air. Two swordsmen moved to meet her, and both lay dead on the ground less than a second later.

Now was my moment. There were three of our hirelings left. Yagmar had predicted that as soon as I began playing, she'd guess what was up.

By then it would be too late.

I struck the first chord, opening the way. Rippling the veil as I had done in retrieving a bar of soap a lifetime ago.

She turned and saw me immediately. She didn't head toward me, though, but back toward the wagon.

Which is why Yagmar now stepped out from cover to block her way. The two with swords moved in behind her, and the crossbowman frantically wound the windlass, loading another bolt.

Yagmar hefted his axe, but she didn't wait for him. She spun back around toward one of the men approaching, and moved, in a great sweeping motion, low to the ground, and he fell in a howl of pain, blood spilling from his leg. Another one out of the fight. With three great steps and a leap, both blades came down on the crossbow man, slicing both his arms and the weapon, and he would never lift another again. That left only one man with a sword, and Yagmar.

It took a few seconds, and that was enough. I reached through the opening I had created, heedless of the mage eaters I could now feel closing in on me. There was a great pain in my arm, but I kept my scream down to a grunt, that I hoped wouldn't be noticed.

It was.

I grabbed hold of the staff and, noticing I'd stopped playing, Niala must have known what was happening.

She abandoned her two foes to sprint in my direction.

The swordsman lunged, and she did nothing but dodge out of his way as she continued.

Yagmar threw his remaining axe.

She tried to dodge that, too, but wasn't fast enough. It caught her in the back. It didn't kill her—I wasn't even sure if it was a serious wound—but it was enough to delay her the half-second it took for Yagmar to catch up to her.

Following the plan, I took hold of the staff, and ran as fast as I could.

"Where do I go with it?" I had asked.

"If we stop her, I'll meet you back at the inn."

"What if you don't stop her?"

"Then you'll have to improvise. Use the staff against her if you can figure out how. Destroy it if you can do that."

Neither sounded like good options.

I ran.

I could hear the sounds of battle behind me as I did.

My left arm was aflame. I could barely move it. I was worried part of the muscle had been torn away. I could fix it, but I'd have to get somewhere safe to do so, and it would take time that I didn't have.

So, I ran.

Forty-One

We All Meet in an Inn

I could see nobody pursuing me by the time I made it back to the inn.

There was no sign of Yagmar or any of the people he'd hired, either. I hoped that didn't mean they'd all been killed.

I ran down the stairs to our room and tried to decide what to do. If Yagmar won the fight, he'd be heading back here. If Niala won the fight, she'd be heading this way, too, eventually. There was nowhere else to go.

I hid the staff, wedging it into the slats under my bed. There was no way I'd be able to unlock its mysteries in the time I had left. Then I went back up to the common room and ordered an ale. I put it on Yagmar's tab. If he was alive, he could pay for it. If he wasn't, then it wouldn't matter.

I sat at the only empty table, watching the doorway, and waiting. I considered trying to flee, but there was nowhere to run to. Impassable mountains to the west. Open desert to the east. Whatever happened, it would be here.

I reached down and felt the bag of rocks I was still carrying inside my tunic. What would happen if I died with all of them on me? Niala had carried them all, though the rules were likely different for a priestess. Which of course made me wonder if I wasn't damning my soul just by carrying them. Did the minions of Arakthala care if the stones were stolen? I thought about returning the bag to my room and hiding it under the bed with the staff.

That thought was banished when the door to the inn opened. The din of the room died off as she entered. Everyone seemed to turn to face her. I rose from my seat.

"Where's the staff, Oghni?" she asked, without even a greeting or anything indicating that she wondered how I got there.

"Where's Yagmar?" I asked her.

"Alive," she said. "Though unhappy. I delayed him a bit, but I don't have a lot of time."

"The staff's gone," I lied. "Beyond your ability to get to it."

"Let me guess," she said, "It's in your room downstairs, tied to the underside of your bed."

Was I that predictable? To cover my embarrassment, I took a step sideways, blocking the stairs to the underground rooms. In hindsight, I can't think of a better way to let her know she was right.

She tilted her head slightly and gave me a crooked smile. Damn her.

I took another step back and stood in the doorway.

"You know I can get by you, right?" she said. It wasn't bluster, just a simple statement of fact.

"Why did you do it?" I asked.

"I'm sorry. There isn't time to explain." She took a step forward.

I drew my dagger, and held it in front of me, in the stance she'd taught me.

She recognized it and shook her head sadly. "Don't make me hurt you, little hunter."

Everyone in the room, innkeeper included, was watching us in silence. None of them stepped forward to interfere.

"Taika's dead," I told her.

She looked down for a second, then back up to meet my gaze.

"I'm sorry," she said again. "I never wanted—"

I cut her off. "He sacrificed himself so we could escape the army, and to send us here ahead of you."

"I figured it had to be something like that. But we're out of time. You need to step aside now." She drew both her daggers. She was really going to attack me. Kill me.

I tried to keep my eyes dry. I didn't succeed.

"I told you not to fall in love, little hunter."

"Do it," I said. "If I'm worth so little to you, just get it over with. The staff is exactly where you said."

She took a step forward.

I could see tears forming in her eyes as well.

The inn door slammed open, and Yagmar stood in the doorway, brandishing his great axe in both hands. "Wanna try this again?"

There was a shocked gasp from the patrons around the room. I'd almost forgotten about them. Hell of a performance we were putting on. If I lived through it, I'd have to remember this, maybe find a troupe of actors to recreate it.

That's what went through my head in the split second before Niala turned, both her knives still in her hands, and lunged toward Yagmar, sliding close to the ground. His axe cleaved the air above her, and her swipe at his ankle missed.

She rolled to her feet and thrust forward at his unprotected back. Yagmar spun out of the way in time, bringing his axe back up and barely missing her on the upswing.

She reached forward again with both knives, hoping to catch his arm between them, but he surprised me by letting go with one, reached over the waiting knives, then let go with the other.

For the tiniest sliver of time, the axe hung in the air before he caught it with the first hand and brought it down again.

Niala turned, blending with the blow as it slid down her bracer and sliced the air between her forearm and her thigh. She swept her leg, caught Yagmar's and he fell to the ground.

Before she could take advantage, though, he rolled away from her and back up to his feet, crashing into an occupied table.

Four men scrambled away, drinks and food scattered behind them.

I cursed myself for a fool and unslung my crwth.

They were nearly equally matched. I could swing the balance. I began playing.

I matched Niala's movements for a moment, as she swung, glided, and dodged. Then, right as Yagmar's axe was swinging down, I played a single discordant note, hoping to interrupt her timing.

It worked, but not as well as I'd hoped. She knew what I was doing and was prepared for it. She moved out of the way, not quite fast enough to stop him from drawing a bead of blood from her exposed upper arm.

She gave a disgusted grunt.

I didn't know if it was aimed at herself for falling for the trick, or at me for pulling it.

I kept playing. Hoping Niala wouldn't notice, I switched my focus to Yagmar.

I gave just a little bit of extra speed to Yagmar's swings, as I had during the fight in the pass.

Again, Niala slid low in front of him, knives extended.

Yagmar brought his axe down, aided by my battlesong.

The axe splintered the edge of a table that Niala had slid close to, deflecting the blow just enough to miss her.

Instead of attacking from there, she rolled under the table, came up on the other side, turned, and pushed it hard with both hands, slamming the table into Yagmar, while ducking low to avoid a one-handed swing of his axe.

She realized what I was doing and was on me a second later. Her knife swung at me in a long arc, and I leaned back to avoid it by a hand span.

Her other knife plunged into my crwth, leaving a trail of blood across my hand as it cut through the strings and shattered the board of the sound chamber. I fell back, and she spun, kicked me hard in the chest before falling to the floor and rolling under Yagmar's axe.

Everything went black for a second and I could feel myself falling into the open stairway but could do nothing to stop it.

Forty-Two
Fight the Future

I opened my eyes and found myself lying halfway down the stairs. My head felt like it wanted to split open.

I could hear a commotion upstairs. I struggled to my feet, no easy task as they were above my head when I started.

When I reached the top of the stairs, I saw Yagmar lying on his back in the doorway, halfway outside the inn. Several people were gathered around him. I guessed from that he was out of the fight, but not dead.

I hoped.

Niala stood there, one arm hanging limply at her side, blood dripping from her bicep. A new scar to show her next lover. Her other hand held a knife and she looked toward me with an expression somewhere between anger and sadness.

Everyone in the small room moved out of her way, giving her a clear path to me. Thanks a lot, guys.

I had lost my dagger somehow, and my crwth was destroyed. It would never play again, and I bit back tears for that as much as everything else.

Even with her injured arm there was no way I could take her in a fair fight. But three older siblings taught me one thing at least: Never fight fair.

My older siblings had taught me a lot of tricks — not all of them by design — but it was my youngest I drew inspiration from this time, as I took another step forward, and took out the bag I'd been carrying with me since we left Rhogna's tomb.

Niala froze as I opened it and pulled out the one I wanted.

"You can't stop me," she said in a soft voice. A statement of fact, not braggadocio. We both knew it to be true.

I dropped the bag to the floor.

Yagmar gasped and I could hear his pain in it. He understood what it was I held in my hand. A black stone, river-polished and painted with intricate designs also all in black.

Niala stopped short, one knife held loosely in her uninjured hand. For a moment we stood frozen, facing each other as blood from our injuries slowly dripped onto the inn floor.

I was barely aware of the crowd around us, staying out of the way. It seemed they were holding their breath as well.

"Please, no, little hunter," Niala said. "There's no coming back from that. If you die while holding that stone…"

"Complete destruction of my soul," I replied, trying my best to keep the anguish I felt out of my voice. "Do you think I'd want to go on to any kind of afterlife, knowing it was you who sent me there?"

There was a kind of gurgling noise from Yagmar. He was trying to struggle to his feet. A couple of people from the inn held him down. If he hadn't been near death, they couldn't have succeeded. He growled in anger, and I couldn't tell if it was directed at the people holding him down, at Niala, or at me for risking such a thing.

Niala slowly raised her knife, into a fighting position. I could tell she was holding back tears as well.

"I need that staff," she said. "Too much depends on it."

"All you have to do is go through me."

"Oghni..."

"Was any of it real?" I asked. The performer side of me cringed at the cliché, but I had to know.

"I told you not to fall in love," she replied, which wasn't an answer.

I honestly couldn't think of anything else to say. I just stared toward her, soul stone held out in my hand.

"I don't want to hurt you," she repeated.

It was too late for that, I thought, but found I couldn't form the words.

For an eternity, we stood, looking into each other's eyes, neither of us spoke. The crowd around us seemed to be holding its breath as well.

"Your soul, against the survival of my people." She took a deep breath and held it for a second. She did let a tear fall, then. "You'll never know how close you came in that balance."

"Wait..." came a hoarse voice from behind her.

Niala jerked forward with the tiniest of movements. As if she had been about to lunge forward, then stopped herself with great force.

She *had* been about to lunge forward, I realized. She was planning on killing me.

I closed my fist around the soul stone and clutched it to my heart. I didn't want to give her an out. If she was going to kill me, she was going to live with the consequences.

Behind Niala, Yagmar slowly pulled himself to his feet, using a broken table leg as a crutch.

"Explain," he said to her.

She turned, so she could keep an eye on both of us.

Logically, this would be the time to rush her, each of us from opposite sides. Right now was the best chance we'd ever have to take her.

Neither of us moved.

"My people didn't hide from the Conqueror. He killed them. We didn't move our villages. He burned them and scattered the ashes to the winds. For a thousand years we've struggled to survive, my people descended from the ones who wouldn't be slaves."

"And what, of any of that, necessitates my death?" I asked her.

"There's a new Conqueror. They're gathering and preparing to invade again. Their hatred of the Shar'i'nol runs deep. They will sweep through the desert, through the remnants of their ancient enemy. With the staff, we will have a fighting chance."

"And without it..." I started.

"We will be obliterated, our resources stripped, my people enslaved to their power, our lives spent in conquest and destruction, as they spread their new empire over the mountains, through Torlindl, and across the sea to the West."

Forty-Three
Blood on the Floor

"So, you're trying to save Torlindl?" Yagmar took a single staggering step forward. One of the men from the inn helped him stay upright. I had seen him in there before, though I couldn't remember his name. An incredibly brave man. I hoped Niala didn't kill him.

She didn't turn to face Yagmar, but kept her eyes on me. *Did she really consider me the bigger threat here?* Yagmar couldn't even stand on his own, and had no weapons to hand, so... maybe.

"No," she admitted. She still kept eye contact with me. "I'm trying to save my people. Torlindl will benefit, but I'd change nothing if they didn't."

The implications of it all were staggering. "You don't... you don't want to attack Torlindl itself?"

"I swear to you, if you put down that stone and let me retrieve the staff, I will never cross the mountains again."

"Why... why didn't you just tell us this to begin with?" I asked. I noticed, though, that her first request was that I put down the stone. I was still angry, and hurt, and most of all, I didn't want to admit to myself that my stratagem had actually worked.

"Veldi would have insisted on taking the staff for herself," Yagmar answered for her, still leaning on the patron.

Niala gave a slight, almost imperceptible, nod.

"You could have told me," I complained.

She gave a sad sort of laugh. "Ironically," she began, "I was trying to avoid hurting you. To not force you to choose sides. If all had gone well—"

I interrupted her. "Well, it didn't."

She looked down, silenced.

Yagmar took a step toward his throwing axe, embedded in a nearby table.

Niala made the slightest movement, a warning, and he came to an abrupt stop.

We were all frozen in place, by stalemate, not truce.

She looked back up at me. "I know. If it's any consolation, I'm sorry."

"What was supposed to happen?" I asked, summoning as much fury as I had left. "You left us to die, trapped behind a portcullis, being attacked by animated statues..."

"They would have stopped as soon as I was away," she said. "I thought the gate would have held for maybe a couple of hours. By then, I'd be on the Tyroth, and away. On foot, you wouldn't be able to catch up. I assumed you'd do the smart thing and give up."

"You forgot to account for the king's army," I told her. "They caught up to us before we could make the crossroads."

"How is that possible? They were days away."

"Not quite as many days as you thought. They were tracking Veldi the whole time," Yagmar finally spoke again. He still didn't move.

She still didn't look at him.

"Taika sacrificed himself to get us away, after they killed Veldi," I said. I don't know why I was explaining it to her. What could I possibly say to change her mind. And... did I want to?

I could see the plan now. Take the staff, steal the tyroth, and run over the mountains. Without mounts, and with winter setting in, we'd be forced to turn back. She didn't count on Lonto being able to get through the gate, or the King's soldiers catching up to us so quickly.

"What do you think, kid?" Yagmar asked. He was still leaning on the unknown man. Now that Taika was gone, was I "kid" again?

Drops of blood still fell to the ground.

I glanced at my hand, where the blood was slowly pooling in my palm. I understood what he was asking.

She had won. We all knew it. There was no sense fighting further. But...

But.

There was only one thing stopping her. My only trick.

As long as I stood in her way, her black stone in my hand, she wouldn't advance.

She hadn't wanted any of this. She cared enough about me to stop. To not destroy my soul when it was the only way forward. To weigh the survival of her people, that she'd been trying to ensure for two centuries, against my own.

She must have still felt for me as much as I for her.

Was it enough?

It would have to be.

I gave the big man the only answer I could. I opened my fist and turned it over, letting the stone fall to the floor.

Niala was moving before it even hit the ground. She picked it up, along with the bag of the others.

"I'm sorry," she said as she passed me. I watched her descend into the darkness below without saying anything.

A moment later she returned, carrying the staff, and walked toward the door. Nobody else had moved.

"I'm sorry," she said, once again, and was gone.

Yagmar did move then, letting his friend help him into a chair. I quickly moved over to him.

My crwth was broken, and without it the spell was more difficult. Heedless of what the locals here might think of the magic, I wove the spell to knit his torn flesh back together. While I worked, someone brought me a clean cloth and wrapped it around my hand, staunching the bleeding.

It would have to do. I could feel the mage eaters pressing around already, and had to stop.

"That's all I can do here," I told him.

"It's enough," he said, standing up. "The rest can heal on its own."

"You can both stay here until you're ready to travel again," the innkeeper spoke. He looked to my instrument, ruined on the floor. "A pity that, but even if you can't afford to pay, the rooms'll just sit empty so you might as well use them."

… Forty-Four

The Shar'i'nol

The next evening, I decided the mage eaters had dissipated enough to try healing again. It was a struggle without my crwth. Taika could have done this in a few seconds.

I spent most of the next eight days in the room or drinking alone in the inn's common room. Yagmar frequently went out, on long walks, but what he did he never said, and I didn't ask.

On the ninth day, there was a knock on the door.

I stood from my chair, where I'd been penning a letter to my sister, and opened it carefully, my knife hidden in my hand, behind the door. Yagmar stood on the far side of the room, a throwing axe in one hand and his great axe in the other.

A man around my age, dressed in a strange flowing outfit with a livery I'd never seen before stood outside the door, holding a large case.

"Are you Oghni of Granjoriil?"

That took me aback. There was only one person in this realm aside from the one in the room with me who would know who I was.

"Who are you?" I asked.

"I am a messenger, from Queen Niala. She bade me deliver this gift, and an invitation to her coronation three days hence."

"Qu... Queen?" I stammered. "Niala?"

"Her *coronation*?" Yagmar bellowed, then threw his head back and laughed. The last time I'd heard him laugh like that we had been lost in the woods.

"How is Niala the queen?" I asked, once he'd settled down.

"A carriage is waiting outside. We can leave immediately if you wish."

"What if we don't wish?"

"She told me if you refused, to suggest you open the gift first. If you still wish to remain, then she will leave you in peace, and reiterate that she has no intention of breaking her promise."

"Oh, this I've got to see," Yagmar said, and stepped forward.

The messenger looked frantically back and forth between us.

"Go wait upstairs," I told him. "Get yourself a drink or something."

"I'm supposed to…"

"Don't waste time arguing about it," Yagmar said. "You can either do what he says or go home without us and then when we show up a day later explain why to your so-called queen."

The messenger left.

"Think it's a trap?" I asked, after taking the package and shutting the door.

"Almost definitely," Yagmar said. "But not the kind where she kills you. If she'd wanted to do that, she could have before she left. Or just sent someone. A queen coulda sent an army to just burn down the whole inn with us in it. No need to lure us into a trap."

"I'm a little worried about her being a queen now. If that's the first thing she used the staff for…"

"Even with the staff, this is a little fast. I suspect something else is up. Maybe she was always the queen."

"That doesn't make sense either. A queen of the Shar'i'nol couldn't just traipse all over Torlindl alone for two hundred years."

I realized I didn't know anything about her position, other than being a "village guardian." She never talked about her family at all. Her travels, her adventures, battles she'd been in, sure. Even a bit about her childhood. I tried to remember everything she'd told me about growing up - privileged, destined, well educated, trained in a variety of arts.

I had imagined some kind of temple upbringing, but a palace would fit as well. I didn't remember her saying anything about the kinds of chores she had to do as a child. Perhaps there were none. Because she was a princess.

"Let's see what's in the package," I said, and laid it on my bed before undoing the twine holding it closed.

I pulled off the wrapping and opened the box underneath.

Inside was a crwth. It was beautiful, exquisitely carved. I'd never seen its like. It was obviously of Shar'i'nol make.

Without speaking, I lifted it from the box, drew the bow and crossed the strings a few times. After spending a bit of time tuning it, I played the one Shar'i'nol song I knew. The one I'd played Niala all that time ago. The crwth had a beautiful rich tone. This was a major step up from the one she had destroyed.

I resisted the urge to smash it into a thousand pieces, and instead set it back in the box.

It was then I noticed the small leather bag.

I pulled it out and opened it.

Yagmar, who had been sitting quietly on the edge of his bed this entire time finally spoke, when he saw what I withdrew from the bag. A river-polished stone, painted in complex designs in violet, gold, and green. She must have finished while crossing the mountains.

"We don't have to go," he said. "These are valuable gifts. You can just keep them and go back across the mountains."

"Is that what you're going to do?"

"I have no plans," he said. "You'll need someone to watch your back, whichever way you go."

"Thanks," I replied, and meant it. "We're going of course."

"Of course."

It wasn't just a carriage that was waiting for us. Three score men and women, soldiers, servants, cooks, and the messenger who commanded them all. I was impressed he delivered both the gift and the message himself instead of delegating it to one of his many underlings.

He didn't speak to us for the duration of the journey. It was only four days. Each night, a small but adequate tent was set up for Yagmar and I, and we dined separate from the retinue.

From what little gossip I could glean, Yagmar may have been right about her already being royalty. Nobody seemed surprised or upset that she'd become queen. Either these were all people who were loyal to her before she left, which seemed unlikely, or it was not an unexpected or resented move for her to take power. Indeed, it seemed they'd long expected it to happen.

We arrived at what seemed to be a temporary encampment. I was expecting an oasis, but I couldn't see any difference between this spot of desert and any other spot of desert we'd traveled through. Large tents sprawled across the desert, arranged in circles around one huge central tent. There were a couple of different enclosures holding their mounts or beasts of burden. I saw no sign of agriculture or shops, but somewhere I could hear the distinct ring of a blacksmith's hammer.

"Your tent is this way," our guide said to us, leading us to one of the smaller tents in the outer ring.

"Remain in here. Food will be brought. You will be sent for in the morning."

"I was hoping to see the Queen tonight," I told him.

"You will be sent for in the morning."

We dropped our bags in the tent, and I washed up in the basin of blessedly cool water they brought us.

"Cold water," I pointed out to Yagmar.

"Excellent," he said.

"I mean, how do they have cold water? Where do they get it from? I didn't see a stream."

"Magic?" He suggested. "That's the first thing I ever saw you do."

I shook my head. "Maybe. But why? Lukewarm would be fine for washing up. Seems an extravagant use of magic."

"We are guests of the queen. Gotta expect some wasteful extravagance."

I heard music coming from somewhere, joined shortly thereafter by someone singing.

I smiled and picked up my new crwth case.

Yagmar laughed softly. "They told us not to go out."

I shrugged. "What are they going to do? They don't need a pretext. If they wanted us dead, they could have just done it any time on the way here."

"Good point," he said, and picked up his axe.

Forty-Five
Where There Be Dragons

I raised an eyebrow at him.

"What, you think I'm going to let you go face all those dangers alone?"

"The dangers of people singing by a campfire?"

"Exactly."

I was surprised at the number of civilians out. This was not a military encampment. Or, if it was, not purely military.

Belief in the west was that the Shar'i'nol were a migratory people. I had heard otherwise long before I met her, and Niala had seemed to indicate I was right. This certainly seemed a temporary, though long term, camp, though. Exactly what I'd expect of someone migrating with the seasons.

There was a small fire — there were actually a lot of small fires — but the one closest to us had half a dozen people sitting around it, one of whom was playing a lyre.

They looked up as we approached.

"May we share your fire?" I asked, in the common tongue. One of them, an elderly woman, said something back to me in a language I didn't understand.

"*Chi-aar, neht sopundois,*" Yagmar replied, in the same language. I guess I shouldn't have been surprised he knew it.

"*Ya-ko saari klupoto!*" the woman said cheerily, gesturing us to empty spots around the fire. I gratefully took a spot.

Twice over the next few hours, soldiers began to approach us — obviously we weren't supposed to be there — but they turned away before making eye contact. None of them were ready to make us their problem.

Other groups wandered over to see the newcomers, though, and soon we had quite a crowd gathered.

None spoke any of the languages I was familiar with, and Yagmar's Shar'i'nol turned out to be fairly rudimentary. I learned that this was a migrating camp, though. They were visiting a series of sacred sites and would stay at each only a few days before moving on to the next. Only a small portion of the nearest village, which was only a few days ride away, were in the camp, and messengers came and went between them daily.

Again, nobody seemed to have any problems with Niala being queen.

"The staff can affect minds," I mused to Yagmar at one point.

"If it could do it to this scale, she'd have used it on us," he replied.

Although the morning's meeting weighed heavily on my mind, I had the first truly enjoyable evening I'd had for a while. It was made even better once someone had brought out the mead. There were several musicians among the travelers, and we had a grand time exchanging songs. I could happily stay with these people for a while.

Eventually, the crowd grew thin, and I made my own excuses and headed to bed.

In the morning, far too early, we were again summoned, with far too much volume and sunlight for my taste, after all the drinking I'd done the night before.

I went to the wash basin to begin washing my face, and one of the soldiers sent to us told me to hurry.

Yagmar, bless him, stepped in again, "We'll go when we're ready."

"It's not wise to keep the queen waiting," the soldier said.

I was about to point out I wasn't even dressed yet. Then I thought about saying something about how it wouldn't be the first time I'd attended to her without getting dressed first. Then I thought better of that.

"She'll wait for us," I told him. "Go outside."

This last, Yagmar emphasized for me with a low growl and a single step forward. The soldier chose the better part of valor and retreated outside our tent.

I deliberately took my time washing up, making sure my outfit was perfect. I slung my new crwth over my back, the way I'd worn its predecessor, forgoing the case. It was a deliberately chosen gesture to be both a token of peace and a reminder.

We followed the soldiers into the large central tent, as I expected.

Inside the tent, more soldiers snapped to attention as we entered. They carried the same ornate pole arms as our escorts. In addition to these, they all wore knives on wrist guards, similar to Niala's.

The royal guard, I assumed. Probably trained to fight in the same style as Niala. Nobody made any attempt to relieve us of our weapons, which was unexpected. I had a whole speech prepared about courtesy to invited guests that now I wasn't going to be able to give them.

The room they led us into was a small antechamber. I wasn't surprised that they would have such a thing in the queen's tent.

What did catch me off guard was when the soldier opened up the inner tent flap and it led not to some inner throne room, but to a stone stairway descending into the ground. Distinctly cool air wafted from the opening, and the aroma of fresh water.

I glanced at Yagmar, and he didn't look like he had been previously aware of this any more than I was.

The soldier stopped at the top of the stairway and nodded for us to proceed without him.

The air grew both cooler and noticeably more humid as we descended. The sound of dripping water came from the distance.

"This explains where the water came from," I said. "There must be an entire lake of it down here."

"Who knows what's underground around here," Yagmar said. "There could be an entire ocean that we don't know of."

"Just the lake, I'm afraid," a familiar voice came out of the darkness ahead.

Niala stepped into view, illuminated by the dim light still streaming down from the opening above.

She had no guards and was dressed in her usual traveling gear.

Yagmar and I exchanged a look.

"You could kill me," she said, "or at least try. Succeed or not, of course, neither of you would leave this camp alive. I hope it doesn't come to that."

"I'd rather not talk of killing," I said. I remembered holding her in our shared bed in the inn at Tuluth. I felt a pang of sadness at the realization that no matter what happened here, I never would do so again.

"Tell us about this lake," Yagmar said.

"Come see," Niala replied, and took a torch from a nearby wall sconce. She lit it, then lifted it up and led us down the passage she had come out of. We wound our way around rocky protrusions in the floor, following a path that may have been originally cut by water. Everything around us gleamed with moisture, and as we proceeded, the sound of dripping water grew louder.

We came to the shore of a lake. The torch light did not extend far, and the lake was lost in the darkness beyond. Water dripped from the ceiling, drops falling from the ends of hundreds of rocky protrusions.

"You see one of the greatest secrets of the Shar'i'nol," Niala said.

I had figured that out already.

"Do any of your people even know this is here? Or do you set up the tent before opening the hidden door in the desert?"

"A few know. The royal guard does. And the Summoner of Cold Water."

"A fancy title for a guy with a bucket?"

"A child. Always a child. They serve for two years and are sworn to secrecy for the rest of their lives. Our leaders are chosen from amongst them. They fill the barrel, roll it to the bottom of the stairs. The royal guard carries it up the stairs, and the child rolls it out of the tent to share with the people."

"Why the elaborate ruse? And why a child, not the queen?"

"I don't know. That's just the way it's always been done. If you're nice, though, I'll let you hear the barrel-rolling song."

Yagmar growled at that.

"He's got a point," I said. "I'm afraid I can never be as nice as I once was."

She looked down but said nothing.

So, I continued, "You brought us here, and showed us this for a reason. What is it? And why are you the queen, anyway?"

"I am queen because the previous queen died while I was away, and the regent recognized me as the new queen when I returned."

Yagmar's hypothesis confirmed.

"But what do you want?" I asked again.

"I told you there was a new conqueror. I need news of him, and my envoys to the East have not returned. The last we heard, he is planning on moving west again."

"What does that have to do with us?" Yagmar asked.

"None of my people who have been sent have returned. Some traders from elsewhere have gone East and come back unscathed, but their reports are unreliable. Whenever anyone from the Shar'i'nol goes, they disappear and are never heard from again."

"So, what, you want information?" I asked. "Hire some of these other traders. You don't need us."

"I need someone I can trust. Someone who can pass borders freely and without suspicion."

At that Yagmar threw his head back and laughed. "After everything you've done, you think we're going to take a job? From you?!"

His laughter echoed through the caves, momentarily drowning out the sound of falling water.

But I already knew I was going to do it. Everything she did was for her people. I couldn't fault her for that. I still loved her, and perhaps someday I'd even find it in me to forgive her. Someday.

"Kid?" Yagmar said, apparently seeing my face. "You can't be serious. We're not going to do this."

"You don't have to go," I said, knowing that he would. But just to make sure, I added with a smile, "If I find you again after I return, I'll let you know about the dragons."

"Fine," he said, with an exaggerated sigh. "But I get my double share this time."

Bonus Short Story: Death of a Young Wizard And What Came After

THE SNOW GAVE WAY to grass as I fell through the portal and went sprawling, landing face down. At some point, I dropped my knife, and there was no telling which world it landed in. That probably saved my life as much as anything.

Under a hot red sun, a heap of snow from my own world landed on and around me, and quickly began melting away.

When I looked up, a strange being stood over me. It was almost human, save for its height, half again my own, bright red skin, and an extra pair of arms just below the ones I would expect. This pair was smaller than the others and the hands held a colorful object, like a small stone, that it was turning over and over. It reminded me a bit of Niala's soul stones, except the colors seemed to shift around as it manipulated them.

In its larger hands, though, it held a long spear-like weapon in a manner which made its intent quite clear. I raised both my hands in surrender, in a manner which I hoped was equally clear.

It wore sewn skins of an animal I couldn't identify. I couldn't tell from any sexual characteristics if it was male or female. Perhaps it was both, or neither, or perhaps its people, whoever they were, didn't even have such a concept.

There were more behind it. A great many more. Many carried spears. The design was unfamiliar, but the purpose obvious. Especially when I saw them in use. I wasn't the only one who had come through the fissure. Scores of other humans, men and women, had fallen through with me. A huge tear hung in the sky, visible to the unaided eye, and snow poured through it. It seemed to be receding as I watched.

The red people with the spears and some other instruments I didn't recognize moved about the fallen. Some, they were herding toward me, some tried to stand and fight them, and were quickly cut down. The red people were brutally efficient.

The one in front of me pointed behind me, obviously wanting me to head in that direction. I tried to stand but couldn't get my feet under me.

It made some kind of fast-paced chittering sound, like "tili-kili-kliki-riki-niki" and pointed more emphatically and leveled its spear at me for good measure.

I tried again, failed again, and nearly broke down crying. "I'm sorry, I can't," I pleaded, hoping it would understand the tone if not the words.

It grunted angrily and put its strange stone away. It bent down, reached out with its lower arms, lifted me and set me on my feet. As soon as it let go, I fell down again, crying out in the pain as my legs gave way. I had used far too much magic earlier today, as I had tried in vain to escape the very soldiers who were dying all around me, and my legs had both been ravaged by the mage eaters. I could tell my ankle and half the bones in my left foot were missing, leaving muscle, cartilage, and nerve but nothing for them to attach to. If it sounds painful, I assure you it was.

It chittered again but put the spear up so it was no longer pointing at me. It motioned with its lower arms for me to stay where I was. It then looked around and, apparently spotting what it was looking for, gave a loud "Hooooo!" call, raising its upper arms high above its head.

A moment later, another one showed up and pulled out another of the strange rocks with the shifting colors. The first pointed down to my foot, and the other touched its rock to it.

Whatever it did, it looked startled. It turned the stone over twice, each time the pattern changed to a different color it leapt to their feet and chittered wildly with the first one. The exchange looked angry, and at one point it tried to grab the spear from the first, who pushed it back angrily and pointed down at me.

Eventually, the second one seemed to relent, took out its magic stone again, and after a few more manipulations, touched it to my leg. My foot and leg went numb. I could feel nothing at all.

That one walked away without a second glance.

The first one again bent down and helped me to my feet. I took a tentative step on my foot and found it could once again hold my weight. I was a little unsteady, nearly falling over again, but at least it didn't hurt.

The creature reached out one of its lower arms and I took hold of it as I walked. I could do it, but it was slow going. At one point, it looked down at me and tapped itself in the chest with a free hand and said, "Nahyej" which I took to be its name.

I repeated the gesture with my free hand and told it my name, "Taika."

"Tai-ka," it repeated.

"Nah-yej," I said, trying to copy its cadence.

It seemed happy at that, and chittered several more things that I couldn't understand.

We came, eventually, to what looked like an encampment. The whole thing was obviously temporary, with tents, garrisons, and three tall wooden towers set up near the edges. Soldiers from my world had begun streaming in as I stumbled in with my captor, Nahyej.

The various soldiers, who I tried not to make eye contact with, were herded or carried into a set of cages inside the encampment, made of a material that may have been some kind of wood. I felt a little bad for the soldiers, having no idea where they were or what was happening. I at least had the advantage of some training in magical arts, so I recognized another world when I saw one, even if I had no idea who our captors were. I felt a little responsible as I was the one who tore open the veil between worlds that pulled them all through to here.

My sympathies for their predicament only went so far, though, as I wouldn't have had to do any of it if they hadn't been trying to kill me and my friends.

When we got to my cage, Nahyej chittered to a nearby red person, who came over, touched another one of those magic rocks to the side and two bars slid up into the top. He pushed me in, not ungently, and the door slid closed behind me. I raised my mage sight and caught a glimpse of something emanating from the stone as the one who opened it placed it back into a pocket. Strangely, I saw nothing on the cage. So all the magic of the mechanism must have been in the stone. Nor did I see any seams in whatever material it was made of.

All that day, I was left alone in my cage wondering what was happening. The soldiers from my world, anywhere from two to four in similar cages to my own, talked amongst themselves, occasionally yelling back and forth between cages. I was kept apart from them and couldn't hear most of what was said. I did gather that they knew who I was and were unhappy with my presence. I resisted the urge to stick out my tongue or waggle my fingers at them.

On the second day, one of our captors brought me a container full of water. It chittered something in its strange language and mimed lifting it to his mouth with his lower hands before handing it to me. I took it and sipped from the container. It was round and smooth and rigid, and I had to use both hands to hold it. I marveled at the gripping strength of their lower hands, which were a bit smaller than my own, but one held the container easily. I shuddered to think of what they could do with the larger ones, which were about twice the size.

It was the first I'd had to drink for more than a day, and I downed it in great gulps. It was room temperature, and I thought of Oghni who had chilled a mug of ale the first time I'd met him. He could cast magic without tearing the veil, just by strategically "rippling" it as he put it. It wasn't an efficient method. It took far more energy for smaller more subtle effects, but it would certainly be handy now.

I could see the veil all around me but could find no way to pierce it. None of the worlds I was familiar with were available to me here, or at least I didn't know how to reach them from this direction. Until I could find a way to do so, all of my magical knowledge was useless, and it was the only thing I was any good at. I'd lost my knife on the way here, but really it wouldn't have done me any good anyway. Even with it, I'd be no match in a fight against any one of the spear-wielding giants, let alone multiples of them.

"Thank you," I said, as I handed the empty container back to my captor, but it again chittered, in a more friendly way it seemed to me. I did so, then asked if I might have something to eat as well. I tried miming the act, using an imaginary plate and fork, but I'm not sure it understood. It just walked away.

A short moment later, there was a commotion near one of the other cages. I looked over that way to see what was going on. It was half hidden behind a tent, but it looked like there were at least two soldiers in another cage and one of them shouted something, then threw a canister of water similar to what I'd been given, through the bars at his captor. He continued yelling, in what I recognized as one of the languages spoken in the far south of my own land, though I didn't recognize any of the words.

I had to admire the commitment, if not the wisdom of his decision. He wouldn't give his captors an inch. When I tore open the veil, my plan was, on the very slim chance I survived, to be captured by these men, who I'd hoped would treat my injuries rather than torture or kill me. I wonder what would have really happened.

Truthfully, I had considered it more likely I would die in the attempt and find myself confronted only by some guide to whatever afterlife I'd earned. Yagmar had put in a good word for me at Ta'va'stok, his people's land of the honored dead. I wondered how many of the soldiers had died. I had believed there to be thousands, but there were perhaps a hundred here, two hundred at the most. I suspected the rest had perished, which made me the most successful killer I'd ever heard of. I felt neither shame nor pride at the thought.

Later that day, when I was getting used to the rumbling in my belly, rather than lie around and moan, I tried walking around my small cage. My legs seemed to be well on the mend. If I'd had access to the worlds I normally did, I could have done it faster myself. With the mage sight, I could see the large rip I'd made in the veil, far away. I imagined it looked smaller than it had, but I knew it could take years, possibly generations, to heal completely.

It was the third day of my captivity. I had lain awake most of the night looking up at a starry sky. There were no moons visible. For them both to be in the new moon phase at the same time was rare, so I surmised this world didn't have them. The stars were similar, but the patterns were all different. None of the familiar constellations were there.

Shortly after dawn, another of my captors came to my cage and handed me a bowl, between the bars. The bowl held some kind of mushy substance, like a porridge or gruel. On top of it was a layer of vegetables of a sort I didn't recognize. There were no utensils, so I dug in greedily with my hands. There was some kind of sauce on top that made the whole thing surprisingly tasty. Or perhaps it was just the hunger, but either way I didn't stop until the bowl was clean. When I looked up, I saw my captor had stood watching me the whole time. It gave a high rapid chitter that I'd learned to take for laughter, when I looked up at it, and took my empty bowl away. Five minutes later, he brought me a new one and I ate it the same way, though more slowly. When I was done, it took that bowl away as well.

Late that night, I was lying on my back, staring up at the night sky. Although hot during the day, it was pleasantly cool at night, so the lack of blankets didn't bother me.

I thought of my first night after the shipwreck, cold and miserable huddled around the fire unable to get dry. Lonto and Veldi, both dead now. Niala turned traitor. I had torn open this passage between worlds in order to send Yagmar and Oghni halfway across our own to catch her. War and destruction of all that I ever loved would be the price of their failure. I expected to die in the attempt, but instead ended up here. I wondered if they were faring any better. If they'd made it across the mountains to the desert.

Three of my captors came together. Two were holding their wicked looking giant spears. The one in front held one of their magic stones in both his lower hands. I switched to mage sight, and saw magical energy emanating from it, as I expected. Tendrils snaked around both his arms and then around his body, up to his head.

One of the ones carrying the spears took another stone and pressed it against the bars of my cage. This time I watched as it reached out, magical tendrils snaking up, surrounding two of the bars and sliding them soundlessly upward.

Without warning, the one in the lead stepped forward and pressed the stone against my forehead. The tendrils snaked out and through and into me. It was not a pleasant sensation. Then he spoke, and it felt like a knife stabbing into my forehead with each word. I yelled in pain and stumbled back, falling to the ground. There was a sound, not through my ears, like a great crowd all talking at once in a thousand languages.

"Wha... what?" I managed to say.

As I spoke, I could see the words, transformed into power, pulse their way through the tendrils into my captor.

And then, they were amplified and pulsed back at me, like someone shouting in my mind.

"Can you understand me?" They said, and I was astonished to realize I could. They weren't the common tongue I was speaking, and they weren't being translated, but I found I could understand them.

"Yes!" I said out loud, and again saw my words pulsing toward the speaker.

"They," and there was little ambiguity that he meant the soldiers, "say you are the one, alone, who created the tear in the sky."

The pain was beginning to subside, though not entirely. It had died down at least enough that I could think through it.

"That is true," I said, not sure where he was going with this.

"They say you killed hundreds of them."

"Good."

"You did not know this?"

"I didn't know how many of them, if any, would die."

"Why did you do this thing?"

"They were trying to kill me and my friends. I was trying to escape."

"Why did you choose my world to escape to?"

"I didn't choose it. When I tore open the veil, I thought only to create a conduit to send my friends far away. I didn't know we would be pulled through to your world."

As I said it, I had a sudden, chilling suspicion.

I had to ask. "Who are you?"

"I am speaker Tinarh. We are the Menders and Protectors of the Sky."

"How... How do you protect the sky?" I asked.

"When demons tear holes in it, we attack the demons. We strike through the rips and pull apart the demons trying to destroy our world."

There was no denying it. "You're the Mage Eaters."

"I do not know this term."

"In our world, we believe you to be the demons, who attack wizards when they're trying to work magic. Our magic involves opening rifts in the veil, reaching into other worlds. We... we had no idea there were people here, or that we were damaging the worlds we reached into. From our side, the tears are small, and mend quickly."

"There are others in your world who do this, then?"

"Yes. They're called wizards. There are hundreds. Possibly thousands."

"They do not mend on their own. Often, when we arrive, the demons flee, and we can work in peace. Sometimes, we must first stop the demons before we can do our work. It will take many of us many years to mend the one you created here."

"I'm sorry. I didn't know. I didn't know there were people in these worlds. I thought them only demons."

"Worlds? Do you tear holes in other worlds beyond our own?"

"Yes. Most wizards know of a few. Some know of dozens. There are probably thousands of other worlds."

"You do not know how many for sure?"

"No. Knowledge of how to reach them is passed from wizard to wizard. There are very few records of them kept."

"I see. We must ponder this."

And, with that, it pulled the stone away and departed, with its two guards.

The sun had risen high in the sky by the time they came back. This world was at least close enough to my own that they had a sun, and the days seemed to be of similar length, though it was hard to tell.

My captor with the translating stone came back. Again, it entered my cell and pressed it to my forehead. I was prepared for the effect this time, and did not reel back.

"I have spoken to our leaders. It has been decided that you were telling the truth."

That was a relief.

"For generations, your wizards have invaded our world, tore your holes, and allowed demons entry, creating havoc across the land. It's rare to capture one whole, though. And unprecedented to have so many come through at once. Our sages believe they can reverse the process by analyzing the magic in your system connecting you to your original world."

"Does this mean you can send me home?" I asked.

"You misunderstand. You shall atone for your crime through your death by dismemberment, which will allow us to open the portal. A grand army, composed of many factions, is being assembled now. We will travel to your world and destroy those you call wizards, and put an end, once and for all, to the destruction you have wrought upon our world, and all the others."

At that, he withdrew the stone, and all of my protestations were for naught.

For the rest of the day, I paced within my small cage. As the sun was nearing the horizon, they began taking the soldiers from my world away. They opened their cages one by one and herded them out, all in the same direction. I wondered what was to become of them. Maybe it had been decided they were innocent in all of this and they were resettling them, or preparing to send them back to their own world, once they'd opened it up. Opened it up by killing me.

I decided that had to be prevented. Not just for my own sake – though now that I had my life back, I was loath to give it up again – but an invasion force of these people, marching on my world, with the goal of killing all the wizards? That was exactly the sort of thing I opened the portal for Yagmar and Oghni to prevent, and why I ended up here in the first place.

I had to do something but had no idea where to start. I was in a cage that I had no idea how to get out of. My magic was denied to me. Yagmar could maybe bend these bars or lift the gate, but my own strength was nowhere near sufficient.

Tired of pacing, I lied down, tried unsuccessfully to nap, then got up and paced some more. Twice they fed me. They were still treating me well, strangely, considering they were planning on later ripping me to shreds so they could destroy my world.

Once the sun had set, I tried again to sleep, laying on my back staring up and the strange stars. I tried making constellations of them: The Musician, the Warrior, the Barbarian. I was trying to figure out which one would be appropriate for Lonto - there was nothing resembling the Bear constellation from my own sky - when I heard very quiet chittering nearby.

I started and looked over, and there lay my original captor, Nahyej. He had crept up along the ground, silently, and I hadn't even noticed he was there until he spoke.

He extended his hand, and I saw a familiar-looking rock held loosely in it. Looking through mage sight, my suspicions were confirmed when I saw the tendrils extending from it to Nahyej and more waving around in the air waiting for me to take hold of it. I did so, bracing myself for the pain.

Nahyej let go of the stone, allowing me to hold it while he spoke. As before, I found I could understand his words.

"Is it true that you are a wizard?" He asked.

"Yes," I replied. Had he come out here just to satisfy his own curiosity?

"And you know how to travel between worlds?"

That was a good question. I told him the truth. "I've done it once."

He was quiet at that for a while. Then he spoke again. "They want to kill you. Then invade your world."

"So I've been told."

"Do you want to leave here and prevent that from happening?"

"Yes!" I said, perhaps a bit too loudly.

"I don't wish them to hear us. Please speak more quietly."

"Sorry," I whispered. "Can you open the cage?"

"I believe so," he said. He pulled out another stone and touched it to the bars. They slid easily upward, as before.

"How did you do that?" I asked.

"I stole the key from the same Mender I stole the translator from. Come, we must make haste. Soon they will discover you are gone, and shortly thereafter, me as well. We must be far away when that happens. We are now both sentenced to death."

I widened my eyes at that revelation, but didn't say anything. I followed after, as quietly as I could, staying low, but I couldn't mimic his gait, running along on all four arms and legs like a giant insect. He stopped, repeatedly, waiting for me to catch up.

Once we were past the edge of the encampment, I broke into a full out run, which seemed to impress him. He stood upright then himself and easily matched my pace.

When we were completely out of sight of the encampment, I stopped, and sat for a moment on a nearby boulder, breathing heavily. He didn't seem winded himself, but was obviously familiar with the concept as he waited patiently for me to catch my breath.

"Why?" I asked him, once I had.

"I have a sibling. They were, or are, a wizard, too."

"I thought you didn't have wizards in your world."

He indicated the stone I was holding. "Somebody made that. Sometimes one arises among us. The Protectors of the Sky hunt them down and slay them."

"And that's what happened to your sibling?"

"I do not know. I have assumed so for many years, but now I think they might not have."

"What changed?"

"You did. When I saw you come through the sky, and when I saw what the damage done to you was, I knew that you were a demon from the other world. Then when you tried to do your magic in the cage, I knew that in your world you must be a wizard."

"But what does that have to do with your sibling maybe being alive?"

"When they left, they told me they were going to learn magic. There is a temple, in an old city, long abandoned and fallen into ruin, where no one may go. We are told it was because of the damage done by the demons. But my sibling was convinced that wizards lived there and that a wizard could get past the barrier."

"Barrier? What kind of barrier?"

"I don't know. But anyone who approaches it is at first pushed backward. They can resist at first, but it gets harder to approach. If they manage to push past it through sheer force of will, then they catch fire and burn."

"You've seen this happen?"

"I have only heard fourth or fifth-hand reports. It's possible that the place doesn't even exist."

"It sounds like wards. I've never been on this side of them before."

He seemed excited about that. "Can you get through them, then?"

"I don't know. Can you take me there? You saved my life and risked yours on the thin hope that I can help you. The least I can do is try."

We traveled through dry rocky terrain, dotted with small bushes, the largest of which were as high as my chest. Nahyej had no map that I ever saw him consult, but he seemed to know where he was going.

I tried the best I could to remember landmarks, mountain shapes, and so on, on the way, but truthfully, I was never really that good at that sort of thing. And I'd only been assuming that the sun rose in the east, set in the west, and the stars made the same journey across the sky.

I asked Nahyej about the moons, and he confirmed he'd never heard of such a thing. There was the sun, and there were stars, and that was it.

Walking all day while my traveling companion hunted, now that was something I was used to. It was hotter and dryer here, though we still had a welcome rain off and on for a few days. I told him of the shipwreck and our long trek through the forest before running into the king's soldiers again. He was fascinated by my description of trees, which he had never seen.

"There were some among the Protectors of the Sky who thought that the soldiers who came through with you should all be put to death."

"They don't deserve that. They were just trying to serve their king. Who knows what lies they were told about us."

"Why did the king want you enough to send an army after you?"

"One of our traveling companions stole something. Something valuable enough that wars would be fought over it."

"That seems to be something our worlds have in common. Powerful people argue with each other, and the rest of us have to pay the price."

I just nodded at that. By now, we had picked up on each other's body language enough for him to understand that much.

It took nearly a fortnight of travel to find the city. There was more left to it than I expected, as if it had been abandoned a few decades, not centuries.

It took the better part of a day searching the city before we found the temple.

It only took an hour of searching the temple before we found the books. They were different from the books I had seen before. The pages were thick leaves of the same material I'd seen in other construction on this world. I imagined from the very shrubs that were now forcing their way through cracks in the city's crumbling roads.

The pages of the books were sewn to each other on alternating sides, so when the book was closed it looked very similar to what I was used to, other than the lack of a spine, but it could be opened so that it formed a single continuous line.

At least, in theory. They were ruined, all of them deliberately torn apart, crushed, and thrown about.

Nahyej looked devastated.

"I have never seen so many books in one place before," he told me. I looked at the mess. There could not have been more than maybe a hundred if they were all reassembled. The library in the dormitory where I lived in Pendwy had that many at least, and that was a tiny fraction of what could be found at the Great Library, which must have had a hundred times as much.

I thought of that library in ruins like this, and realized his people would do exactly that if they had a chance.

"They did this. When they were just beginning. Fifty years ago, maybe, they did this. This was not the work of demons. It was the Menders and the Protectors of the Sky."

He looked through the books, picking them up one by one. He handed me one, "Look!" he cried. "This is about creating an opening to another world! Is there anything in here that can help you?"

I looked at it, but the symbols on the pages made no sense to me.

"I cannot read it," I told him. "I guess the translator stone only works on spoken language."

He dropped the book to the ground and sat down, holding his head in his upper hands, weeping. "So much destroyed. So much taken away." His gesture took in the grand city, now in ruins. "All hope is lost."

I picked the book up, then opened his bag and put it inside.

He just looked at me as I did so.

"Not yet," I told him. "I cannot read the words *yet*, but you can teach me. You said there are other cities?" He nodded. "Then we'll find them. We'll find those hidden wizards. I don't know if I can ever find my way back to my own world, but somewhere out there is the knowledge we need to save yours. Together, we will find it."

Yagmar and Ogni's adventures will continue in Yagmar the Barbarian and the Demons of Azhkarrakil, coming soon!

Printed in the USA
CPSIA information can be obtained
at www.ICGtesting.com
LVHW020205241124
797243LV00010B/334